He was o [illegible] rger, more robus [illegible] d as though he b [illegible] wam in the seas. He wore eelskin clothing of an antique style and a green hooded cloak.

As they watched, he opened a pouch at his belt and took out an object that glowed with steady light.

"What could that glowing thing be, a lamp?" asked one worker of another.

"If he needs a lamp by daylight, there's something wrong with his mind," the second worker replied with a laugh.

"You're both fools," said another of their companions. "The Old Storytellers told of his coming. That is his sign. The Eye of the Dragon!"

Books in the SCORPIO Series from Ace

SCORPIO
SCORPIO RISING
SCORPIO DESCENDING
DRAGON'S BLOOD
DRAGON'S EYE

DRAGON'S EYE

Alex McDonough

A Byron Preiss Visual Publications, Inc. Book

ACE BOOKS, NEW YORK

This book is an Ace original edition, and has never been previously published.

DRAGON'S EYE

An Ace Book / published by arrangement with
Byron Preiss Visual Publications, Inc.

PRINTING HISTORY
Ace edition / September 1992

Developed by Byron Preiss.

Editor: John Betancourt.
Cover painting by Kevin Johnson.
Book design by Dean Motter.
Special thanks to Janet Fox.

ISBN: 0-441-75513-5

Ace Books are published by The Berkley Publishing Group,
200 Madison Avenue, New York, New York 10016.

PRINTED IN THE UNITED STATES OF AMERICA

10 9 8 7 6 5 4 3 2 1

DRAGON'S EYE

Chapter
1

Leah held her breath as the orb-craft she rode in touched ground as softly as a bubble. Its walls of coruscating light began to grow filmy and insubstantial. She knew they had reached their destination, wherever that was. With Scorpio's piloting anything was possible. She tried to pull the safety and non-being of orb space around her like a sleeper trying to hide from morning in his blankets. Soon sights and sounds would crowd in.

With a shock she saw the strange being who shared the craft with her. He was tall and gaunt with gray skin and a frightening face; a single facial bone created a beak above his lipless mouth. Only the eyes were comforting. They were large and blue-green with a vulnerable look. It wasn't so much Scorpio's appearance that shocked her after all their travels together. Orb travel created a mind-link between the two of them. When they reached a world, she was always surprised to see that Scorpio was an entity separate from herself. She knew that the mind-link would rapidly fade once the orb bubble burst, leaving their mutual telepathic powers somewhat sketchy. Now, however, as the scene beyond the orb wall began to come clear, she was perfectly aware of his thoughts and feelings. She could feel his uncertainty, mingled with hope that he had at last mastered the orb. Beneath everything was his desire to finally see his homeworld of Terrapin again. He had left his people, the Aquay, under the tryannical rule of the fierce Hunters. Throughout their travels, he had never stopped thinking of the Aquay and hoping that he could somehow help them.

Out of the clearing haze Leah began to recognize landmarks. St.-Bénézet's Bridge spanned the gunmetal-blue water of the Rhône River. Twenty-two arches of roughhewn stone extended into murky distance over a half-mile span. Hordes of people passed in the street on their way to cross the river. Raggedly dressed peasants with sunburned faces, prosperous-looking burghers and artisans, here and there a noble of the court, dressed in a silken mantle and fashionable long-toed shoes. Couriers darted among them and peddlers jostled and cried their wares. In short, a street scene that Leah had seen a thousand times without really seeing it at all.

On the opposite bank was the Palace of the Popes. It was impressive in scale but except for narrow trefoiled Gothic windows and two slender spires framing the main gate, it was otherwise without ornamentation. It sat haughtily on a rocky outcropping, the Rocher des Doms, overlooking the city. Avignon itself clung to the hills like honeycomb, a collection of shining whitewashed structures beneath red tile roofs.

"I'm home," said Leah softly as she recognized familiar landmarks. She felt Scorpio's satisfaction. In their travels a landing was always made with a sense of dread because Scorpio's control of the orb was incomplete, to say the least. The device had been stolen from his enemies, the Hunters, as a last act of desperation. As they traveled, he had been learning, though, and now he had brought Leah back to the place where he had found her.

Time seemed extended as Leah stared at the bridge and the structures beyond. She had often marveled at the famous Pont d'Avignon, a feat of engineering considered a miracle, but now there was something about it that bothered her. Since animals, oxen and horses, were a part of the traffic, the unpaved streets were littered with dung and other debris. In the heat of afternoon a stench hung in the air. She remembered the folk tale of the villein, leading some donkeys, who walked down the lane of the perfumers' shops. Instantly he fainted at the unaccustomed scents. Townsmen brought him to by holding a shovelful of manure under his nose.

The usual pack of beggars lounged at the near end of the bridge, noisily soliciting passersby. Leah knew that many of them were "false beggars," a missing arm bound tight under a shirt, perfectly sharp eyes under a blind man's ragged bandages. Their filthy rags and raucous voices created an aura of sleaziness. Also, Leah couldn't escape the feeling that the bridge was somehow smaller, less impressive than she remembered it. Of course, now she knew that in future ages putting a bridge across even the widest river was commonplace.

Leah's concentration was broken as a boy with a grimy face pointed at her and jabbered excitedly. Not only had Avignon appeared to them, Scorpio and Leah were on display. When the orb bubble burst, the orb itself had reformed into its usual smaller shape and lay at Scorpio's feet.

"We'd better get moving," she said, taking Scorpio's arm. "The sight of you is likely to cause trouble." Then she looked down at herself and remembered that she was wearing a bizarre costume from the twentieth century—jacket and trousers, just like a man. Scorpio gave out his low warbling laugh as he scooped up the orb and followed her lead as she began to work her way through the crowd. But Leah knew there was nothing funny about appearing out of nowhere in an outlandish costume in an era that took sorcery literally and punished it by death. She remembered that her father had been accused of using sorcery to murder Cardinal de Gascon. She herself had been under suspicion of sorcery as her father's assistant. The fears of the superstitious were pretty much confirmed when she and Scorpio disappeared.

They negotiated narrow streets, made dark by the overhang of roofs and odorous by the emptying of slops into the gutters. The smell of the city wasn't something Leah had never noticed, but it was now more obvious because cities of the future didn't take filth for granted. They turned down shoemaker's lane. Tradesmen of the same sort tended to cluster their shops along the same street, so there was a butcher's row, street of glass workers and so forth. The shops were merely horizontal doors let down from the houses' facades, forming a counter. Shoemakers and their apprentices were on display inside as they plied their trade. Occasionally, when the crowd thickened, the apprentices would come outside and turn salesmen, not only shouting the praises of their own master's wares, but denigrating the products of the shop next door. They did everything but drag potential customers bodily over to the store.

As Scorpio and Leah darted into a side street to get away from a gang of children that had been chasing them, shouting epithets and throwing clods of dung, Leah saw that a housewife had hung her laundry on a wall in the sun to dry. She grabbed several garments nearest her and bundling them under her arm began to run. She ran faster when she heard a shrill female voice shouting, "Thief, thief!" Scorpio pounded along behind her. At last when it was obvious that there was no pursuit, they stopped in a cul de sac where overlapping buildings created a shelter. It occurred to her that the old Leah who had once walked along these byways would be shocked at the idea of so casually appropriating someone's clothing. But the old Leah didn't have any idea of the importance of looking exactly like everyone else.

Leah spread the garments on the cobbles to see what they had. Among her haul she found two *pelissons*, a sort of loose, robelike all-purpose garment and two *bliauts* or overtunics. They were of rough wool homespun, much patched and mended, but she supposed they would do. She would use a length of cloth as a girdle to give her own outfit a more feminine look. They took turns using the sheltered nook between buildings to change their clothes. Even though the fabric was still damp and clung to her skin, Leah felt better in the familiar garment. "This isn't going to disguise my face," said Scorpio, emerging.

"Here, try this," said Leah. She presented him with a *chaperon,* a combination cap and cape, and helped him pull it on over his head. It stuck up in a peak at the back of his head but covered cheeks and shoulders. Since the *chaperon* was a dull blue, Leah saw that Scorpio's face took on a definite bluish cast. His skin tended to take on the color of whatever garment he wore. Seeing that strange blue face would give someone quite a shock; luckily the only part of his face that could be seen was through a slit in the front.

In these disguises they could travel on unimpeded and

Leah turned toward the Jewish quarter where she and her family had lived.

"What's the great hurry?" asked Scorpio.

Leah looked around. She had set such a brisk pace, she was almost leaving Scorpio behind. By the ringing of the bells, which were rung every three hours marking the offices of the church, and the position of the sun, she judged it was about midafternoon. Time suddenly seemed very important.

"I'm sorry," said Leah, "I guess I'm just anxious to get home again, to see if it's there, just as I remember."

"You're not certain I got the time right, is that it?"

"You have to admit that your control hasn't been all that good before. I've seen enough landmarks in the city to know that this is the Avignon I remember, so I know where we are but I'm not sure exactly when we are."

"You wanted the time that you lost so I attempted to bring us back to a time shortly after the Pope's men chased us and forced us to use the orb to escape. I think I managed to do it."

"We can't be sure until I find someone I know. It's not a good idea to just ask a passerby the month and year. We're already suspicious-looking enough."

"You know that the orb wouldn't allow me to enter a time where you and I were present. It has something to do with protecting our minds from the overload of paradox. Since we weren't here during those ten years, the orb allowed us to come back."

Leah remembered. Because Scorpio had no control, the orb had hopped through time and brought them back to Avignon ten years after her father's execution. It had been very strange to talk to a childhood friend who was years older than herself, but the most frustrating of all was that she was helpless to aid her father. She had tried so hard to clear his name and find the real murderer, but though she and Scorpio had tricked the real killer into confessing the deed to Pope Clement, the Pope had refused to make public that it was one of his own cardinals who had committed murder.

From time to time in her travels, she had dwelt upon the injustice of it. Not only was an innocent man executed, but by the time she found out about it, he was ten years dead. It was this that preyed upon her mind as she hurried toward the Jewish quarter.

"I know you want to go directly to your house," said Scorpio, "but we'd probably better not. If I really managed to bring us back to the proper time, there may be guardsmen about searching for us."

The Jewish quarter was surrounded by a high wall and accessible through a toll gate. As they approached the gate, Scorpio paused. "What if the gateman recognizes us?" he asked. "Isn't he likely to report it to the authorities?"

"I don't have any *sous*, either, for the toll," said Leah, "but I think I can figure something else out." They strolled along the wall for some time, Leah looking this way and that. A boy had once bragged to her that there was a way in and out without bothering to use the gate and he had told her the location, though she had never had an opportunity or inclination to put his information to the test.

"Look," she said, pausing by a huge oak tree whose trunk had grown into the stones of the wall. The warped trunk and extending branches offered a rude staircase up the side of the wall, for anyone agile enough to use it. She and Scorpio climbed it, letting themselves down inside on a springy branch. Leah supposed that to get out again, it would be possible to leap up and drag down a branch and then shinny along it like a monkey. It wasn't the kind of thing she would have thought of doing as the daughter of the eminent Doctor Nathan de Bernay.

The streets and byways of the Jewish quarter were every bit as narrow and winding as those of the rest of Avignon, but they were slightly cleaner, as the rabbis were more stringent about sanitation laws ignored in other parts of the city. She now felt calmer as she saw the small but well-kept houses like her own, each with a mezuzah nailed to the doorpost. It was easier to accept that she actually was home, after her travels through time, but at the back of her mind the sense of time fleeting still remained.

They approached Leah's house cautiously. There seemed no movement about, but it might be a trap. Leah circled about and, seeing nothing threatening, walked through the kitchen garden and entered through the back door, exactly as she had often done after an errand for her father or Grandmère Zarah. The kitchen was in disarray, table and benches overturned, the larder ransacked and emptied, as if whoever waited here had grown bored and hungry. The remains of their impromptu meals lay scattered on the floor.

Leah couldn't help thinking how her grandmother had held sway in the kitchen, making sure the bare board floors were brushed clean, the utensils that hung at hearthside shone with polishing. Leah had spent many happy hours here, the hearth glowing, the air filled with the smells of Grandmère Zarah's good cooking. Though in her travels she had seen empires fall and kings overthrown, the tyranny of time hit her most strongly here. A person's life's work could be cast down in a matter of hours or days.

Scorpio moved about nervously, but to Leah the house held a pervasive atmosphere of abandonment. If the

Pope's men had searched here, they had come and gone, and now were likely seeking them in other places.

Even though she knew it would be painful, she looked into her father's study. The desk where he had pored over his texts had been overturned. Precious herbs and nostrums he had spent so much time gathering lay scattered. She stepped into the room, her mind filled with memories of working with her father here. Suddenly someone grabbed her from behind.

She didn't even have time to scream before she saw Scorpio leap forward, taking one of the odd fighting stances he had learned in their travels in Cambodia. His hand shot out past Leah's head and made contact with her attacker. She felt herself released so suddenly, she staggered forward. When she turned she saw Scorpio standing over a fallen enemy.

"Scorpio, stop!" she shouted before he could strike again. "It's Mossé, my father's friend."

Mossé, who was a stocky, muscular man, looked puzzled as to how the gaunt Scorpio could have laid him low so quickly, but he was struggling to rise and fight again, until he recognized Leah.

"You're alive!" said Mossé. "After all the rumors I hardly knew what to believe."

Leah came to help him rise. "After the Pope's men left, Rabbi Lunel posted me here to guard against other intruders," he explained and then he looked at Scorpio. "How did you learn to fight like that?"

"It's not fighting," said Scorpio. "It's a philosophy."

"Remind me not to argue philosophy with you," said Mossé with a grin.

"If the Pope's men were just here seeking us, we may still be in time," interrupted Leah. "Do you have any news of my father?"

"Yes, but it's not good news," said Mossé. "Despite our efforts to clear Doctor de Bernay's name, Pope Clement has sentenced him to hang in a week."

"You did it," she said, turning to Scorpio. "We're here, and there's still time to rescue my father."

"That would be too dangerous," said Mossé. "Even if I could raise a troop of men, we'd be no match for the Pope's guard."

"You've done enough for me, Mossé," said Leah gently. "I couldn't ask you to risk your life or the lives of your friends. But now that I know that we've come in time, I'd like to see Grandmère Zarah if that's possible. Do you know where she is?"

"She's staying with the Morels for the time being. This has all been very hard on her at her age; she's quite ill. Even though an old woman is no threat, the Pope's men may still be watching for you and Scorpio to return. They must know you're still alive, even though rumors have spread that you were drowned or killed by the guardsmen."

Leah glanced over at Scorpio. He carried the orb beneath his *pelisson* where it protruded like a small potbelly. "We have a way to get to the house unnoticed."

"Be careful, then," warned Mossé. "It's dangerous for her as well as for yourselves."

"Thanks for your help," said Leah as they turned to go.

She had considered looking into her own room, but now it didn't matter. Now that she knew they were in time, there were plans to make. The small room where a young girl hid her treasures and dreamed of the future wasn't all that important. Not only had she seen the future, she was determined to change it.

"So that was why you asked to be brought back to this particular time," said Scorpio.

"I know that ten years from now my father is dead," said Leah, "but in this time he's still alive. Do you think there's any chance of changing the future?"

"Remember that I don't really know that much about the orb, or about time, for that matter," said Scorpio. "It may be that since your father is dead ten years from now, that we tried to rescue him and failed, or maybe there are other futures—maybe even one where he was saved."

Leah put her hands to her temples. "Don't talk about those things. It's all too complicated; it gives me a headache. All I can concentrate on is now."

"It would be easy enough to use the orb to bring him out of the Pope's dungeon," said Scorpio. "I could simply materialize inside the cell, and—"

"I thought of that, of course," said Leah, "but doing that would make him a fugitive. We know well enough what sort of life that is. I'd rather figure out a way to make Clement keep his word and release him with a full pardon."

That evening Scorpio and Leah crouched in the shrubbery outside of the house of Jean Morel. To avoid getting the Morels in trouble, Leah had decided to wait until the family was retired for the night and make her visit a secret one. She knew there was a small spare bedroom in the loft, so she supposed that was where Grandmère Zarah was staying.

After a while the soft glow of candlelight from inside the house was extinguished. Scorpio removed the orb from beneath his garment. It cast an aura of golden radiance that Leah tried to shield with her hands for fear anyone watching or passing by might see it. "I think they must all be asleep by now," she whispered. "Let's go in."

They clasped the orb between them and were quickly transported to the loft bedroom. Leah heard Scorpio grunt as his head bumped the low ceiling. By the light of the orb Leah could make out various shapes in the room—a square boxlike one that must have been a chest, the low bed, occupied now, the sleeper an anonymous mound beneath the coverlet. Leah went to the bed and knelt beside it, as Scorpio stood behind her. "Grandmère Zarah," she said gently.

The coverlet stirred. Grandmère Zarah's wrinkled hands pushed the blankets aside. She peered out, blinking against the light that was cast by the orb. Leah had always remembered her as strong, but now she appeared frail. She squinted at Leah as if trying to see her. Leah remembered that Zarah's eyesight had been fading. She couldn't be sure she was recognized. She reached out and took Zarah's hand in both of hers. "It's me, Leah," she said.

"Yes, my granddaughter, Leah. It's so good to see you."

"I've heard you weren't well."

"The Morels were kind to take me in and to care for me, but it's not like having your own home, your own family."

Leah said nothing at first. She knew she was in no position to take Grandmère Zarah home, to care for her, not with the Pope's guard seeking her everywhere as a sorceress. "I love you, Grandmère," she said at last because that was all she could say.

"I love you too, child," said Zarah. "I know you're dead, but it's a comfort that you can still come to me in dreams."

Leah released the frail hand she held and let the old woman get back to her sleep. There wasn't any use in upsetting her further. *Why not let her think my appearance was only a dream,* Leah thought. *Even with all my plans to alter time, maybe I am as insubstantial as a dream.*

"Let's go," she whispered to Scorpio, and reached out for the orb.

In seconds they stood outside the house again. "I'm glad I could see her," said Leah, "even though I can't do anything to help her."

"You'll be helping her enough by rescuing your father," said Scorpio.

"If it can be done," replied Leah.

Chapter 2

Pope Clement VI paced his gorgeously appointed apartments high in the Magna Turra, the Great Tower of the palace. He had just asked a servitor for his favorite dish, fresh trout in wine sauce, only to be told there was none available. He knew that in a pond in the palace gardens several species of fish were cultivated just for this purpose, but the man had told him there was something wrong with the pond—that all the fish were found floating.

The impudent wretch had been sent scurrying away under orders to find a fresh trout somewhere or to look to the safety of his immortal soul. But now that he thought about it, it wasn't just the loss of a tasty meal that troubled him. He had been told that Leah de Bernay and the creature that accompanied her dived into the fishpond and had not come to the surface. Since it wasn't all that deep, several guards had dived in, too, only to find that by some means their quarry had escaped. That had made gossip throughout the court for days. Only now were things getting back to normal.

Too much of a supernatural nature had taken place here, for that matter. Saints and miracles were all right for feast days, but became unsettling as a part of everyday life. It had all started when those two red devils had appeared here in his chambers, to tempt him with their golden orb.

Since things so often went Clement's way, even a minor incident like not having a trout for supper put him in an ill humor. He called for his serving man and ordered him to prepare the steam bath on the lower floor. He needed something to calm his nerves. He'd be glad when the whole problem with de Bernay was over. With the execution scheduled for the end of the week, things would soon be set right, despite the usual protests in the Jewish quarter. Nothing could go wrong now. Clement had made sure that the story would not get out. Still, it did bother him that no trace had ever been found of Leah or her demonic companion. That was one loose end that he wished he could tie up.

An hour later Clement ascended the stairs to his bedchamber, his corpulent body wrapped in a huge towel. The steam bath had left his skin pink and glowing, and hairless as he was, he resembled a giant infant escaped from his cradle, his blanket wrapped loosely around him. His serving man padded along behind carrying an oil lamp. Despite attempts at luxury, there was something inherently austere about the Gothic style of architecture. Tiny trefoil windows high up on the tower wall let in thin streams of moonlight, but the staircase was narrow and dark. The cold of stone seeped into Clement's bones despite the warming he had just had in the bath.

His chambers, too, were high-ceilinged and echoing,

devoid of warmth, despite the many frescoes of human activity—hunters after a boar, fishermen drawing their nets, young women and children picking berries in the forest. He had commissioned these scenes by the court painter Matteo Giovanetti de Viturbo in an attempt to bring him closer to life, but the scenes only underscored the fact that he was, of necessity, cloistered here, away from humanity. The sumptuous apartments, thick tower walls around him and above him, and archers pacing the tower's perimeters could make him feel physically safe, but as one who was promoted as spiritually perfect, even he sometimes had doubts and fears when it came to mortality and the worlds beyond.

Well, a goblet of good red wine before retiring should make things all right again.

He was about to enter his robing room when he thought the light of the lamp flared. When he turned to look, he saw the backside of the fleeing servant and a circle of golden light hovering in the air. Inside it, like a chick in an egg, was one of the red devils.

Stunned by this sudden appearance, Pope Clement almost let the towel drop. He recovered it just in time as the golden bubble dropped to the floor and there burst, leaving the devil standing before him.

It didn't escape Clement's notice that this devil was somewhat the worse for wear. His face was crisscrossed with scars, the skin peeling. The black cloak he wore was tattered at its edges and the leather skullcap scuffed and worn. Despite the fact that it had only been a few days ago that he saw the same creature healthy and neatly garbed, it looked as if the thing had traveled for leagues on foot and without provisions.

If it hadn't been for feelings of vulnerability because of his undressed state and thoughts of mortality, Clement's first act would have been to summon the guard. In their earlier visits these red devils had caused him a great deal of trouble. After all, what would be thought of a pope who consorted with something so devil-like?

Still, his earlier musings left room for doubt. Worlds other than this one might be ultimately unknowable. This appearance was surely as wondrous as any saint's miracle. Also, the orb the being carried, now grown small enough to lie on the palm of his hand, still glowed with a steady light. Clement had coveted it before and it still caught his eye.

"If you call for aid, you'll regret it," said the being. There was something in his voice that hadn't been there before, a desperation that gave his words weight. Clement remembered that when the being had appeared before, he had been self-assured and impudent as if the universe belonged to him. Something had happened in his travels to change that attitude. Clement would never know what it was, but he knew that what he faced here was an outré version of a cornered rat.

"None need know of your presence, save myself," said Clement, trying to choose his words carefully but drafts playing through the chamber made him shiver. "Please, may I enter my robing chamber and dress more appropriately for your visit?"

The thing gave a grunt that Clement took for acquiescence, but it followed him into the robing chamber and watched as he pulled on a dressing gown heavy with ermine tippits. "I was about to ring for the servant and order a goblet of mulled wine and honey cakes," said Clement. "Would you accept my hospitality?"

"Order what you like," said the being. "Your wine would burn my throat. I'll remain in hiding here, but remember that I'll be watching you and the wrong move could mean your death." Clement saw that the thing carried no bow or pike. He was unaware of any other weapons in this world that could kill at a distance, but he was inclined to take the being at his word.

After the refreshments had been ordered and delivered, Clement motioned his guest to a seat beside the bedroom hearth that blazed cheerily. Beginning to feel a little more confident as he ate and drank, Clement said, "It's odd you should have appeared to me tonight. My mind was much on otherworldly matters." He offered a honey cake and the being turned it over and over in his thick red fingers and finally crammed the dainty morsel into his mouth. He warded off Clement's offer of wine.

The creature made another noise, but this was a sibilant buzzing, like bees in a hive. Clement finally decided it was laughter, of a sort.

"You know a great deal about other worlds, do you," said the creature.

"It's my job to know," said the Pope, "though I'm always ready to learn more. What sort of being are you? And why have you sought me out?"

"I am Lethor the Hunter," said the creature. "Assassin of the first rank." When he said this he pulled himself up taller and attempted to straighten his tattered cloak. "When we were here before we learned that you imprisoned the male parent of Leah. Since they have come back here, the reason seemed obvious. 'To find prey, it's not always necessary to have it in sight,' " Lethor said, the last sounding like an aphorism.

"So you've come for my help," said Clement.

Again the sizzling, half-suppressed sound of laughter. Though it was supposed to convey mirth, it gave Clement a chill. "Yes, I've come for your help," said Lethor, the irony in his voice apparent even to Clement. "Is there any reason you can't give it?"

"None, none," said Clement soothingly. "This place you come from, is it, well, hot?" Clement was beginning to feel a nagging sense of guilt.

"It's *very* hot on my homeworld," said Lethor, his eyes going dreamy in the firelight. "None of this 'water from the sky' that burns the skin. Since I left home I've been in nothing but barbaric places. I'll be very glad to finally kill this Scorpio so I can go home again."

Despite the troubling detail that the being came from a hot place, Clement sensed a weariness, almost a despair that was human enough to be reassuring.

"They are my enemies, too," said Clement. "The girl Leah caused a great deal of trouble when I arrested her father. It was even worse when she escaped my men. Tales of her sorcery swept the city. When nothing came of it, the wild rumors died down, but now you say she has returned. We will make a pact to wait for them together. When the evil Scorpio is destroyed, you will have two orbs of power. Perhaps if I prove a friend, you might reward me with one of them."

"If you give your help, it would be only just," said Lethor, and Clement heard no irony in the voice. Something in the alien's weariness made him vulnerable, if only fleetingly.

"I will put Nathan de Bernay's cell under heavy guard," said Clement.

"No. Don't give them a warning. When they use the orb, I will know it." He looked down at his own orb as if he could read some sign in its steady light.

"That's better yet. You can take full advantage of my hospitality. I live well here, you'll see."

Clement was awake long after he had drawn the damask curtains of his elegant bed. He wondered if there was some remote possibility that this being was really from hell, sent here to tempt him. He pondered it for long hours, but at last the pragmatic side won out and by morning he was snoring loudly and comfortably.

Lethor the Hunter also stayed awake well into the night, but this was because Hunters needed less sleep than humans. They slept in short stretches in keeping with their predatory beginnings. After he had been shown to the guest chambers, he used the orb to move about the palace and the cathedral that abutted it. He stood now high above the nave of the Cathedral Notre Dame-de-Doms.

Mankind had labored like ants on this structure, finding ways to build ever higher in stone. Moonlight poured down on him through the tall stained-glass window that portrayed the miracle of the loaves and the fishes, striping him with bands of color. *All this labor; what is it for?* He had been in this age long enough to have some idea that it was a religious activity. A monument in stone to their insignificant God. But he gathered they had an imperfect notion of what this God was like. For example, they had never asked Him directly if He wished all this time and effort to go into a useless stone building. What was the point of a God that didn't walk right up to you and make His demands known?

It was all so barbaric it made him want to laugh, but

there was still an atmosphere in this immense building that didn't lend itself to laughter. *Still, imagine that fool of a Pope thinking he could be an ally of a Hunter.* Of course, it was easier for Lethor if that was what he thought. Like all the primitives, Clement was gullible and believed that he would be rewarded by one of the sacred orbs. It didn't hurt matters that in his superstitious way Clement believed that Lethor somehow fit into his crude idea of how the universe worked. He gathered Clement believed him to be some sort of evil spirit. That was good. It would tend to keep him in line.

As soon as Scorpio was properly dispensed with, Lethor would rid himself of the pesky humans as well. Leah, who had no idea of the dangers of getting between Hunters and their prey and the Pope who thought himself important enough to wield a sacred orb. As he looked down at the orb, he felt a touch of fear. For a moment it had seemed to pulse with varicolored light. *My imagination,* he thought relievedly, looking up at the stained-glass window. *That must have been where the colored light came from.* He had reason to worry about the orb's condition, for though he had believed nothing could affect the orb's magic, in a cold climate its light had gone out. Lethor didn't like to remember that time. His Beta companion Ardon had died because of the orb's failure. He had almost been killed himself.

But the orb only glowed serenely now. Nothing was wrong. Toward midnight, he returned to the rich chambers and bed the Pope had provided. Lethor told himself that he wasn't impressed much by what these primitives considered luxuries, but the bed was very soft, the hangings around it filtering out all noise. He checked the beam weapon on his wrist in case Clement decided to rethink his bargain. The power capsules in it were his last. With the orb he could return home for refills, but to do so would be to be questioned by Prime as to why the Aquay wasn't already dead. *It has been a long chase,* he thought, his mind roving over the times and places where he had followed Scorpio. *Surely now the chase will come to an end.*

Leah turned about before the huge mirror admiring her finery. She wore a close-fitting gown of gray silk with sleeves edged in sable that hung to the ground. Over it she wore a black tunic embroidered with wild strawberries. Actually, it wasn't her finery. The clothes belonged to a royal guest of Pope Clement. She and Scorpio had hopped from room to room until they had found garments they liked. From far off she heard the delicate music of the festivities that had been in full swing when she and Scorpio arrived in the palace. She had suggested finding disguises since it would be easier to find and speak to Clement if they looked like guests.

"Aren't you ready yet?" asked Scorpio. He had decided that a monk's hooded robe had served him well as a disguise here before and would do so again. A number of monks helped with the serving, so he would blend in, even if he didn't match Leah's splendor. She was now rummaging in an ivory casque and a moment later brought out a pendant set with an immense ruby. "There. Just the thing," she said, putting it around her neck.

"Do you think you should?" asked Scorpio. "Isn't that valuable?"

"I'm not stealing it," said Leah. "Only borrowing. It is handy to have the orb to take us wherever we want to go. We can be in and out before anyone knows we're here."

"The Hunter may know we're here," said Scorpio. "Haven't you noticed that he always seems to find us when the orb is in use?"

"Well, we won't be here long, anyway." She set an ornate headdress set with gold and pearls on her head, letting the long black gauze veil trail across the lower part of her face. "Let's go."

As Scorpio began to activate the orb, it faltered. Its usual golden light fragmented into prismatic colors that played across Leah's and Scorpio's faces. "What's wrong with it? It's blinding me," said Leah.

"I don't know," said Scorpio. "I've only just learned to control it. It's never done this before." As they watched, the whirl of colors began to dim until the light subsided into dull gold again.

"Thank goodness it's all right," said Leah. "We'd have been stuck here in this room with no way to explain our presence."

"It seems to be back to normal now. Maybe we'd better go," said Scorpio.

The orb deposited them in the main dining hall where the Pope's guests were just arising from the banquet. The orchestra playing in the next room invited them to take part in the dance. Scorpio and Leah mingled with the crowd of guests and servants moving toward the next room. The ballroom was immense, its vaulted ceiling held up by rows of columns. Far off, at the other side of the room, was a dais with several seats on it. Clement would no doubt occupy this place of honor, though for now the seats were empty.

Leah let herself look around and enjoy the sight of rich

wall hangings, the elegant costumes of courtiers and guests. Leah had always heard tales of life in Clement's court, and had wondered what it would be like to be a fine lady. The orb made it easy to seem to belong here. *No one will give me a second look,* she thought, *and Scorpio should be all right if he keeps the cowl pulled about his face.*

After a few moments she realized that it wasn't quite true that no one would give her a second look. Several young men of the court turned their heads as she walked past. Of course she hadn't come here with romance in mind, but it was still flattering.

As the orchestra struck up a tune, men and women paired off and began to dance. The dancing, where men and women actually touched, was scandalous to Leah, but still she watched, fascinated. A moment later a tall figure stepped in front of her, doffing his cap and making a low bow. "Would you do me the honor?" he asked.

Leah was about to decline when she recognized the man, Aimeric de la Val d'Ouvèze. He was the courtier she had once thought she was in love with until she found out what he was really like. Since the surprise of seeing him left her speechless, he must have supposed that silence meant assent. He boldly took her hand and led her onto the dance floor.

To bolt for the sidelines would have drawn too much attention to herself. "I'm sorry, I'm unfamiliar with this dance," said Leah, hoping to excuse herself politely.

"I can't believe that one as lovely as you doesn't spend all her hours dancing," said Aimeric. "But it's no matter, these are easy steps. Follow my lead."

It was true that the steps were easy to follow, but Leah now saw that Pope Clement was taking his place on the dais. This was the perfect time to confront him, since to call out his guard would spoil the party. In the throngs she had lost sight of Scorpio. Several monks moved among the guests serving refreshments.

Aimeric had been speaking, but Leah didn't know what he had said. It probably didn't matter since it was probably more mindless flattery. He was flushed from the dancing and wore a handsome surcoat of dark blue velvet and a soft cap of gray leather. His hose displayed well-formed legs. Leah could well believe that once she had admired him and had dreamed of being in such a situation as this.

Now that she was, she could only wait impatiently until the dance ended, so that she could escape from his banal conversation. What she had to do was more important than childish daydreams.

He'll probably be glad to be quit of me as well, she thought, *since I've only been half listening to him.*

"We must dance again," he said as the music ended.

"I'm afraid I'm too weary," she said.

"Fine, I'll get you some wine and wait until you've rested," he said. "I don't intend to let you out of my sight until I've convinced you to lower your veil and let me see your beauty entire."

"Wine, yes, that's a good idea. Get some at once."

He led her to a gilded bench. "Stay right here; I won't have to go far."

For all he knows my face is pockmarked beneath the veil, Leah thought. Still, she couldn't help feeling flattered. Somewhere in her travels the old naive Leah had been lost; Aimeric must have sensed the difference and been fascinated by it.

As he went off to get the wine, she got up from the bench and began to work her way across the crowded floor toward the dais. Scorpio might be there already, wondering what had delayed her.

Chapter 3

Scorpio fidgeted as he waited for Leah. Disguised as a servant he couldn't loiter around for long without someone noticing. Earlier he had seen someone on the dance floor that resembled Leah, yet he must have been mistaken since she hadn't come here to dance. She was too serious about her purpose to rescue her father.

Scorpio hadn't admitted it to her, but he wondered about the possibilities of changing events in time that had already taken place. Since the orb wouldn't let its user return to a time where he was likely to meet himself, that might be its way of preventing paradoxes. Changing an event that had already happened could cause differences to occur down the timestream. Still, minor events were scarcely ripples in the overall flow, so maybe saving the life of one individual really didn't matter that much.

Despite his worries, Scorpio was willing to go along with her plan because it was the key to reestablishing Leah in a happy life in her own time period. He owed her that much. He owed her more, he realized, but knowing she was safe in her own time would allow him to get on with his mission. The Hunters had invaded his world and were killing and enslaving his people, and now that he had some control of the orb, he might be able to help them. He supposed he would be impatient to get away, except that impatience had no meaning to a time traveler.

This adventure in Avignon might prove useful at that, he thought, if it taught him more about the nature of time and the powers of the orb. "Sir, more wine here," said a guest, already too tipsy to see that Scorpio carried no tray.

"Yes, right away," said Scorpio and to avoid trouble, he found a door behind the dais, and still reassuring the guest that he was going for wine, he backed through it. He found himself in a small well-appointed anteroom and turning about he saw a table laden with all kinds of fancy dishes. Behind the table engrossed in his eating sat Lethor the Hunter.

"I knew you'd come," said Lethor, as though he had sat here waiting for just this opportunity. The grease on his chin indicated otherwise. "My orb sensed that yours was in use." He placed his orb on the tabletop. Scorpio felt his own orb stir where he had hidden it in his voluminous sleeve. There was definitely an affinity between orbs that allowed the Hunter to track them.

Lethor lifted his right wrist, the one that bore what looked like a black plastic bracelet. "I'd say that this was a great triumph," said Lethor, "but all I feel right now is relief."

"So you and Pope Clement have become allies," said Scorpio, trying to think of anything to create a diversion. He couldn't activate the orb quickly enough to avoid the weapon's beam unless he somehow distracted Lethor.

"Allies." The room buzzed with sinister laughter. "The

man is my slave. He begged to help me, to offer me his full hospitality. My near-vision confirmed that he was telling the truth."

Scorpio knew that evolution had given the Hunters a sort of telescopic vision and it might be used to scan a person's face as he spoke. Liars gave telltale signs, a twitch of the lips, a tic in the eyelid.

"Pope Clement is a cold man who has had a lifetime to practice his trickery. Otherwise he wouldn't be in this high office. Leah believed him too when he promised to free her father. He betrayed her even as he gave her reassuring promises. Do not trust him or you'll be sorry for it."

"What can he do to me? I have the orb." As he touched it, he drew back his hand. Crazy patterns of colored light played across the walls. This would have been exactly the distraction Scorpio wanted, except that he felt his own orb move inside his sleeve and in a very unorblike manner begin to wriggle between his arm and the cloth until it rolled out onto the floor. Scorpio's own orb was also strobing with prismatic light.

Scorpio saw Lethor reach futilely for his orb as it rolled across the table and bounced onto the floor. The two orbs moved closer together, light flaring and growing more intense. Both Scorpio and Lethor were forced to cover their eyes as the room filled with light.

When the light faded, both orbs were gone.

Ignoring Scorpio, Lethor crawled around the room, looking under furniture. "Where did they go?" he asked plaintively.

"You know more of the devices than I do," said Scorpio, "but both seemed very excited. Do you know anything about the mating rituals of the things?"

"That's disgusting," said Lethor.

"Perhaps, but do you have a better explanation?"

"I don't want to hear that about the all-powerful orb," said Lethor. He turned away, still in search of the missing orb; Scorpio finally used the distraction to make a break for the door. He heard a thin whine as Lethor activated the beam weapon, but seconds later he was out the door and zigzagging into the crowd.

He slid to a stop as he saw that Leah was on the dais beside Pope Clement. She was speaking earnestly. She must have waited for Scorpio but when he didn't appear, she started without him.

"So you refuse to pardon my father," Leah was saying as Scorpio climbed onto the dais. "Here's my friend now. He's the possessor of a powerful talisman. It was through this that we escaped your men. With it we can carry you off in plain sight of your guard and all your guests."

Scorpio went to stand beside Leah without saying anything. The Pope didn't know the orb was missing any more than Leah did. Maybe he would capitulate.

"Lethor!" shouted Clement. "They are here! I have drawn them out, just as I promised."

"Scorpio, your orb! Show this tyrant that we're serious," said Leah.

Scorpio couldn't see Lethor exactly, but he could see a tumult among the guests, people struggling to get out of the way, others thrown bodily aside as Lethor made a path through the crowd.

"I don't have the orb," Scorpio said in a whisper.

"What?" asked Leah.

"I don't have it," he said more loudly.

A beam of red light shot over the heads of the crowd and burned a wavy line in the bare stone of the wall behind the dais. Leah and Scorpio exchanged looks and began to run. They were half carried through the doors by fleeing nobles and servants. The disturbance among the guests gave them just enough of a distraction so that the Pope's guard didn't reach them, and so that Lethor had no clear line of fire. Or at least Scorpio supposed that was the case, since there were no more bolts of light.

"We got in so easily," said Leah. "Getting out may be a problem without the orb. What happened to it?"

"I'm not sure," said Scorpio.

When they reached the great, ornate doors of the front entrance, they saw that two pikemen stood guard inside. *There are likely more outside,* Scorpio decided, *but one problem at a time.*

"My lady has fallen ill from eating too much at the banquet," said Scorpio. "I was told to escort her home."

With a bored air, one of the guards leaned his pike against the wall and opened the door to let them pass. A shout came from behind them. "Stop those two; they are assassins!"

Scorpio grabbed up the pike and spun it two-handed, testing its weight. He gave the man at the door a sharp jab in the ribs with the blunt end, doubling him over, just as he whirled and caught two of the oncoming men off guard. He sent them flying as he grabbed Leah's hand and led her out the door.

Outside, a guard stood holding the bridle of an immense dapple gray destrier. Scorpio swung the pike and the man let go of the bridle and fell backward trying to get out of the way. Grasping the ornate caparison, Leah managed to climb up and she put down a hand to help Scorpio. He was only halfway there when several more guards burst from the doorway shouting. The war-horse, with nothing to hold him back, bolted, iron-shod hooves pounding.

For a moment Scorpio swung dizzily alongside, and

then he managed to find purchase with his hands and feet in the ornate trappings. Leah was bouncing crazily in the saddle and struggling to grasp the reins.

"Don't slow him down," panted Scorpio. "They'll probably come after us."

"I couldn't, even if I wanted to," said Leah. She had the reins, but her arms were corded from tugging at them, even as the huge beast galloped on.

She wasn't able to exert control, but finally the horse turned into a side street and was forced to stop when the byway came to a dead end. Scorpio and Leah both tumbled into the mud and offal of the unpaved street.

"Are you all right?" Scorpio asked. He couldn't see Leah in the unlit street.

"I'm fine, but my clothes are ruined," said Leah.

Scorpio's warbling laugh rang out. "They weren't yours to begin with. Are we still pursued?"

Both of them were quiet for a few minutes, listening for the shouts, the sounds of running feet. Except for the barking of a dog, the streets were silent.

"Now," said Leah, "you must explain to me how you lost the orb."

"I didn't lose it exactly," said Scorpio and told her the story of how both orbs had disappeared in a burst of light. "What was really odd was that the Hunter didn't have any more idea than I had what was happening. You'd think if the Hunters discovered or invented the orbs, they'd know how they work. Lethor was offended when I mentioned that the orbs might be doing the equivalent of mating. It was only a wild guess."

"If the orbs disappeared, that means they could have gone anywhere. Do you think they'll be back?"

"Would you, if you'd found the sphere of your dreams?"

"I guess there's no way to predict what it'll do now," said Leah, "which means we have to change our plans."

No magic? I guess that means we think of something else, thought Scorpio. Leah's practical nature continually amazed him. She was ready now to take on time single-handed. *If I'm to help my people, maybe I'd better learn from her,* he thought. *When this part of the journey is over and she remains in her own time, I wonder how I'll be able to go on without her. She's not water-born, not Aquay, but we've shared so much.*

Leah had called together a few of her friends from the Jewish quarter to discuss plans for attempting to free her father. "I didn't think I'd have to call on you for help," said Leah, "but time is growing short. My father is to be executed in a few days."

"We're glad to do anything to help you and Nathan," said Guillaume Morel, one of her father's old friends.

"I thought the best thing to do first is for me to meet with the leaders of the Jewish community. I'll get out the word as soon as possible."

Guillaume looked shocked. "No, you must let me handle that."

She suddenly realized that she was in the fourteenth century. Women weren't leaders here. Her father had made her feel important by allowing her to assist him, but if she had never time-traveled, she would probably have managed to conform to the rules of her society. Her travels had changed her thinking. It was painful to think that she could not handle this campaign herself, but must use a male go-between.

Still, she thought. *This isn't about me; it's about my father. I'll handle this any way it has to be done.*

"Yes, of course that would be best, Guillaume," she

said, though her words had an edge that none of them noticed, except perhaps Scorpio, seated beside her.

"We have already begun some protests on Nathan's behalf," said Mossé. "Word spreads quickly in the Jewish quarter."

"I know that everyone here is doing all they can," said Leah, "and I'd like to extend the campaign beyond the Jewish quarter. It's just too easy for the Pope to consider this a Jewish issue and ignore it."

"It *is* a Jewish issue, isn't it?" asked Mossé.

"Tyranny is an issue for every free person," said Leah.

Her friends exchanged puzzled glances, then she realized that these people had known nothing except the tyranny of kings and popes for generations. She sighed. "This is going to be harder than I thought," she whispered to Scorpio.

"I thought perhaps we might print up leaflets, posters, take them city-wide," said Leah, again getting a blank stare. "I know they would all have to be produced by hand and it would take a long time, but—"

"Your father taught you to read, Leah, because he was learned," said Mossé gently, "but do you know how rare a skill that is in this city?"

"All right, then we'll spread the word orally. The beggars on the bridge who tell the tale of its building hold travelers spellbound."

"That's only so that accomplices can slip up behind them and cut their purses," someone said with a laugh.

"We will steal something more valuable—their hearts and minds," said Leah. "We will organize as many storytellers as possible and send them throughout the city to plead the case of the innocent Doctor Nathan de Bernay."

Leah felt exhausted as the meeting broke up. "I feel

like a fool," she said to Scorpio. "Trying to use methods that haven't been invented yet."

"I think you did pretty well," said Scorpio.

"I guess the only thing to do is to persevere and use what is at hand," said Leah.

The first reports Leah received about her campaign were optimistic. Protests continued to explode throughout the Jewish quarter and word was also spreading through the rest of the city. Leah began to feel better.

She and Scorpio had established headquarters at the de Bernay house, when a courier came in with news. "Our storytellers are being arrested," he said between gasps for breath. Scorpio helped him to a chair. "The Pope's guard is swarming all over the city. It will soon be too dangerous to assemble a crowd."

"I should have realized that Clement wouldn't sit by and do nothing," said Leah. "Call them back. I don't want to be the cause of wholesale slaughter."

When the courier had gone, Leah slumped into the chair. "We're defeated," she said, "and time is running out."

Scorpio tried to console her, but he could do nothing. He decided to go into the kitchen and make them something to eat. At least that would be doing something practical.

As he stood in the kitchen, Scorpio saw a flare of light as if a lamp had been lit behind him, but he knew there was no lamp. Afraid to hope, he turned around.

"The orb," he said. "It's returned to me." The orb lay in the middle of the dusty floor as if it had never been gone.

"Is it your orb?" asked Leah, who had heard his cry and come into the kitchen. "It looks different somehow."

It was the same slightly mottled spheroid but it was

half again as large as it had been, and the light it gave off was more intense, a whiter gold. "I think so, but it is bigger," said Scorpio uncertainly.

"You said the orbs seemed to be mating," said Leah. "Could it be with child?"

"It seems more like the two orbs merged," said Scorpio.

"Well, it doesn't matter, does it, as long as it's back and it works the way it used to. Tomorrow is the execution. We can still rescue my father tonight. The life of a fugitive is better than no life at all."

Scorpio knelt and picked the orb up gently. "Let's see if it still works. I'll take us to the Palace of the Popes."

As a new reality formed about him, Scorpio realized they were in a large, dimly lit chamber. A bed was in one corner, the silken hangings drawn about it.

"I thought we were going to my father's cell."

"I thought so, too. Maybe I don't have the control I thought." For all its elegant appointments, the room had a strangely quiet, gloomy atmosphere. The two low-burning tapers were the only source of light. "Or maybe there's some reason the orb brought us here," said Scorpio.

"The bed curtains are closed," said Leah, "as if the bed is occupied, but no one has challenged us for being here. A deep sleeper or—"

Scorpio pulled back the curtain and suppressed a cry as he recognized the figure stretched out on the bed. At first he thought the Hunter was only sleeping, and his reflexes prepared him to run. Then he realized the figure was too still.

Lethor had an oddly peaceful look on his alien face.

Scorpio briefly inspected the body. "No mark on him," he observed.

"I believe that poison is the usual means of disposing of an enemy in this court," said Leah.

"But he was a guest," said Scorpio.

"Maybe it became too embarrassing to have something so demonlike around," said Leah.

"First the orb returned to me, and then to him," said Scorpio. "It must be a combination of the two orbs."

"But it returned too late to do him any good," said Leah with a shiver. "I don't like this place. It has too many secrets. Let's rescue my father and get away from here quickly."

"We can't go without at least saying a few words over him before committing him to The Deeps."

"Isn't that hypocritical considering that our lives are a lot safer now that he's dead?"

"It's important," said Scorpio.

"All right, if you have to, but be brief."

Scorpio began to intone a singsong chant in his light, warbling voice.

> "Seafaring soul,
> Good thoughts speed your journey
> Into The Deeps where the Eye
> Of Raniki never blinks.
> Sail away rocked slowly,
> Safely, forever in your cradle-boat."

Leah looked anxious as Scorpio took his time over the closing of the bed curtains. "I can't wait to see my father's face when he sees us, when we tell him that he's to be freed."

The cell was in contrast to the room they had just left. Narrow and dank, the rock walls bulged inward as if to remind the prisoner of their substance. Trickles of water ran down their sides into the filthy straw of the floor. Except for the orb the place was in darkness. They could hear the jangle of a chain as someone moved about. Leah bit her lip to think of her father in this awful place. Scorpio held out the orb before him and they could make out the shape of the prisoner, a round-shouldered dejected silhouette, too dispirited to even turn about at the unaccustomed burst of light.

Leah was about to run to him when she realized that the form was subtly wrong. She saw that into the back of his head was shaved the shape of a cross, as was often done to madmen to invoke the Lord's blessing. When the man turned, she wasn't surprised that it wasn't her father. His face was pale and flaccid, unlined and devoid of expression.

"Have we gotten the wrong cell?" asked Scorpio.

"No, this was where they were holding my father before. Unless they moved him, or—Oh, Scorpio, didn't I just say that Clement had a way of removing anything that might be an embarrassment."

"Wait here," said Scorpio. "We'll get to the bottom of it."

It seemed the orb light had hardly faded when Scorpio was back again, this time accompanied by a beefy man in the livery of the Pope's guard.

Of course the man was terrified since one minute he had been on watch, the next in this filthy cell. He threw himself on his knees before Scorpio and begged for his life.

"I'll spare your life if you tell me what happened to Doctor de Bernay," said Scorpio. "And what this man is doing in his place."

"He was killed," said the guard, "weeks ago. It wasn't my fault. Just orders." The guard's eyes protruded wildly and he groveled in the straw. Scorpio lifted him up and gave him a brisk shake.

"Just tell us what we want to know."

"I don't know the reasons. You think he would tell me? Maybe he was afraid this de Bernay fellow would smuggle his story out. Anyway, he was silenced. This lunatic took his place. He's the right size and all. Nobody's going to know the difference since he'll be hanged with a covering over his face. And it isn't the first time something like this has happened, I can tell you."

"Too late," said Leah in a muffled voice. "If only we had come earlier."

"Tell me," said Scorpio, "exactly when was he killed?"

Leah burst into tears when the guard mentioned the date. It was the day after she had last visited him in prison. Since the orb would not let them return to a point where they already were present, they had arrived too late to save him.

"We must go," said Scorpio. "We can't be discovered here."

She didn't answer, but only stood there numbly. Scorpio closed her unresisting hand over the orb and they jumped.

Leah wasn't even aware that the orb-craft had landed. They were on a street in Avignon, but it was pitch-dark, so she had no idea exactly where they were. Only a few pinpoint lights were visible through leaded-glass windowpanes and the miasma of the street rose about them. To Leah it now felt like an alien place.

She became aware that Scorpio was extending the orb toward her. "This helped you to overcome your grief once. It has the healing touch."

"No . . . no, thank you," she said, the words sounding coldly formal even to herself. "That's too easy. I should have accepted my father's death a long time ago, but the orb gave me false hopes. I should have known it was folly to think I could change something that had already taken place."

"We would have changed it," said Scorpio stubbornly, "if it weren't for Clement's perfidy. Who would have known he'd do such a thing."

"Don't you see, there was never any chance of changing it."

"But it's not as you think," said Scorpio. "Events in time are not fixed."

He had to think that way, Leah realized, because he still hoped to save his people. From their brief orb journey, when their minds melded, she could still feel his anxiety over being away. Of course it conflicted with his desire to see her safe and happy here.

"There's only one answer to our dilemma," said Leah. "I must go with you."

"I couldn't. You don't know what it's like to be so different from everyone around you, to be so easily dismissed as a monster before anyone takes the time to know you as you really are."

"Have you forgotten I grew up in the Jewish quarter?"

"After what's happened you're thinking of me and not yourself," said Scorpio. "You don't believe it's possible for a single person to affect time. You want to be there to comfort me when I fail."

"It's hard to keep secrets when our minds interlink in orb space," said Leah, brightening just a little. "If what you want to do is possible, you'll need every advantage. If I can be of any help at all, even just moral support, you must take me along."

"All right," said Scorpio. He didn't take too much convincing since she knew he had never really wanted to leave her in Avignon. She felt the same. Even though he was an alien, she had never had a better friend than Scorpio.

Chapter 4

Yan trudged between monotonous rows of leatherleaf, spotting occasional weeds and rooting them out with a tool like a long-handled trowel. Waves of heat and dust rose from the sandy soil, giving a nightmare cast to the arid landscape. Overhead the sun glared down from a broad expanse of cloudless sky, but to the west boiled masses of thunderclouds with lightning flashing from within. The Hunters' forcewall kept clouds from passing over, creating an unnatural strip of desert on an otherwise watery world.

Yan gave the roiling thunderclouds and driving rain that fell constantly beyond the forcewall scarcely a glance. Yan was an emaciated figure as he strode between rows, flesh weathered close to the bone, his skin a chalky gray. The dry climate made his large eyes rheumy and red-rimmed.

His desultory progress through the field was speeded up when he heard the dull *thrup-thrup* sound of a Hunter's hovercraft. It was a clumsy, slow-moving vehicle, but it allowed a few overseers to inspect miles of cropland. Yan knew that the Hunters monitored the growth and harvest of leatherleaf carefully, and that there must be some product connected with it. Tons of the stuff was evidently shipped to Chanamek each year, but he knew little about why they found it so useful.

As the Hunter passed overhead Yan busied himself at digging out a particularly stubborn clump of weeds. Despite the distance, Yan knew he was being minutely scrutinized by the Hunter overseer. Their eyes were equipped with the power to bring far things near.

Yan squinted up into the glare of sun and saw the figure in the craft's gondola, black cloak flying, horned head silhouetted against a brassy sky. He felt little for the Hunter except a mild curiosity. He realized that the Hunters ruled the compound where he lived and enforced this tedious work, but as long as he could remember, this had been the life of the Aquay.

He relaxed again as the *thrup-thrup* sound dwindled with distance and he fell into a rhythm—walk a few paces, stab at a weed. The field was only occasionally broken by outcroppings of striated rock. As he approached one of these, he startled a long-lizard that had been sunning its snakelike body. It half ran, half slithered into its burrow at the base of the rocks. A few minutes later he heard a sharp cry from overhead and felt rather than saw a hovering shadow. The huge bird hung suspended in the still air. An unnatural shape. The creaugh had pulled its head back into its chest cavity as it soared, leaving a headless silhouette to haunt the skies. Yan wished he hadn't seen the thing. The creaugh was an omen of death to the Hunters.

All of the creatures in this desert world had been transplanted here by the Hunters. Yan supposed they wanted a place where they could feel at home, but he had heard rumors that this narrow foothold of desert was only the beginning, that they were building a device to drain the oceans of Terrapin by spraying the water into space. But there had always been rumors since the invasion, so who knew what the Hunters were really capable of. Not that there was anything he or any other Aquay could do to change things.

With the heat and the monotonous labor, the day seemed to stretch out interminably, yet eventually the sun began to decline behind the massed wall of storm clouds to the west. Yan had only just shouldered his weeder and was turning back toward the compound when he began to feel that he was being watched again. He thought that perhaps the Hunter had returned, but there was no fluttering sound of the hovercraft. As he looked up, he felt he was seeing a mirage. The sun had split into two, large and small globes of golden light. He wiped his eyes. The long workday in the hot sun must be having its effect. The second and smaller sun hovered there for several minutes and then blinked out of existence. That made Yan certain that he had become overheated and was seeing things. He hurried toward the compound. He could just catch a glimpse of the faceted buildings glittering in the sun's last rays. As he came closer, he met other Aquay who had been tending crops. He saw Voce walking along casually as if their paths would bisect by accident. She was as thin and pale-skinned as himself, but there was still a glamor about her in his eyes. The angle at which she held her head, the sway of her shoulders as she walked, fascinated him. He could only see this from the corner of his eyes because he dared not look at her directly in case a Hunter was about. The Aquay were forbidden any lasting emotional attachments, but Yan and Voce had naturally gravitated toward each other since childhood. At the Choosing

Voce had selected Yan after seeming to consider others. Yan had been jealous even though he knew that ultimately she would choose him.

"Will you see them?" said Voce in scarcely more than a whisper.

Yan made the head-tossing Aquay sign of assent and Voce moved away, joining another group making its way to one of the females' dormitories. He wished she could have stayed with him as he entered the Aquarium. Once inside, he passed between rows of immense tanks. Yan felt his dry skin twitch as he saw the cool green water, the aquatic plants. Sometimes in dreams he felt himself completely immersed in water; he must have been remembering his days as a fry.

The tanks were a nursery for numerous Aquay fry. Children were water-born and for the first ten years of their lives they were completely aquatic, breathing by means of a series of gill slits on their torsos. The fry looked like miniature adults, except for a few differences. The webs between their elongated fingers and toes were thicker and more pronounced. The feet were angled straight back, the ankles immovable, making walking impossible. Between their shoulder blades was a small fleshy triangular fin. During metamorphosis, the gills would seal shut, forcing the fry to breathe air. Gradually, the swimming webs shrank, the ankles and feet changed position, and the dorsal fin was absorbed.

As Yan stood looking into the tank, three fry came to hover just inside the glass. He could see a family resemblance, and he supposed the fry could, as well. It was rumored that once families had lived together in half-submerged cities, but now females and males were segregated in dorms, except during the Choosing. Fry were kept in these tanks until they grew larger and were sent off to Chanamek for education. Grown children were never sent back to the compound they came from, so Yan would never get to meet them.

The three fry bumped against the glass of the tank, bubbles rising from their gills. Yan touched the surface of the glass and found it cold. After a moment he moved on, pretending to look at other fry. Parents weren't supposed to try to identify offspring, but he knew of others who came here to see fry they recognized as their own. He wished he could come here with Voce, but they only dared come separately. If the Hunters realized they recognized their children and still felt something for each other, they would be sent to different compounds.

Leaving the nursery complex, Yan walked wearily to the workers' barracks where he shared a room with several others. His quarters were dark as he entered except for a rippling reflection on the walls that told him his roommates were watching watervision. The screen filled half of one wall and the pictures that played there would have been singularly boring to any being except an Aquay. Endless images of water in all its forms moved before the Aquay's eyes as they sat immobile. Waterfalls gushed over high cliffs, monotonous waves moved against a sandy shore, underwater settings with shoals of fish and waving seaweed mesmerized the watchers.

Occasionally this entertainment was supplanted by a short public service message in which a stern-faced Hunter urged ever greater efforts toward bringing in a successful leatherleaf crop, or some similar exhortation. During these brief breaks the watchers usually lost interest, disappeared into the kitchen to fix a snack or into the bathroom. When the scenes of running, leaping, surging or placid water returned, so did the Aquay.

Yan joined the others. After his long day of toil it was

good to just sit back and imagine that he was floating in all that water.

Leah and Scorpio came out of orb space beside a shallow sea where conical shapes thrust from the water. Their surfaces glistened in the sun, for they were composed of thousands of tiny, iridescent shells.

Leah was glad the landscape had changed from that of arid land planted in endless rows of a black, leathery plant. Scorpio was silent, as if brooding over the future of his race. "I know we Aquay tend to be timid by nature and not the best fighters, but I thought we had more spirit than this."

"They've probably been through many privations," said Leah, hoping to cheer him up. The Aquay they had seen were like automatons, fulfilling the Hunters' program as if they had never known freedom. Leah felt that it was probably an impossible task to instill any sort of spirit into those robotlike figures toiling in the sun, but for Scorpio's sake she had to try.

"I don't understand it," said Scorpio. "It's as if all traces of self-esteem and hope have been leeched away. I don't know how such a thing could happen."

"Where are we now?" asked Leah, hoping to divert his attention from such gloomy thoughts.

"This is Hsarlik, the Beautiful City," said Scorpio. "Here the Aquay live as they were meant to."

"But when are we?" asked Leah, looking up at a sky filled with clouds. "The Hunters haven't set up their forcewall in this time."

"No, this is about five hundred years before the Hunters arrived. We're here to talk to someone who should be able to help us, Verlane, the TimeKeeper."

"Yes, I got that much from your thoughts. This Verlane

is a historian of sorts, but I'm not sure why we need him. We have the orb to go when and where we choose."

"After seeing the fate of my race," said Scorpio, "I have to believe the past can be changed to affect the future. But it's not possible to effect any change without knowing the past."

"Why wouldn't you know the history of your race?" asked Leah. "It's important."

"I know that now, but we fry didn't realize at the time that there could be any practical application to learning about a lot of dead people and events long past. I'm afraid I spent too much time daydreaming while the teacher lectured."

Leah cringed as Scorpio led the way into shallow, tepid water. After a while the muddy bottom dropped away, and they swam the short distance to Hsarlik.

"Can you find the TimeKeeper?" asked Leah as she paddled about in the wide canal that served as the city's main thoroughfare.

Scorpio pointed to a building that overtopped the others around it. "By the sign graven into that tower, this is the Great Library. Verlane founded it and was reported to have spent much time working on his studies there."

"It's easier to find the Library than the door to enter by," said Leah.

"That's not so hard if you're an Aquay," said Scorpio. "All our entrances are from below. We'll have to dive." He stretched out his hand to her. Scorpio was a much stronger swimmer than Leah. With him holding her hand and pulling her along, they dived deep. When she opened her eyes again, she saw an opening in the shell-encrusted structure before her. Water pressure thundered in her ears. She worried for a minute whether a human could hold her breath long enough to enter an Aquay door and then they were through, heading for the surface.

Leah came up spitting water, and found herself in a large chamber whose floor was of water. The walls were covered in a layer of sea-grass, dyed and woven into attractive patterns. A floating tabletop on which sat a vase of some sort of flowering seaweed drifted by. They hadn't been there long when a boat came through an archway and moved toward them. Though the boat was small it contained a tall chair. A dignified-looking Aquay in a vestlike garment with shiny gold buttons sat on the chair and poled the craft along.

"Who is calling and what is your errand?" asked the Aquay.

"I wish to talk with Verlane, the TimeKeeper. I am Scorpio, a seeker of knowledge," said Scorpio. Though this sounded like a ritual, the boatman was still staring at Leah, which made Scorpio add, "And my trusted companion."

The boatman looked at Scorpio suspiciously, but was evidently too polite to remark on Leah's hairiness and strange features.

Finally seeming to decide that despite her appearance she posed no threat, the boatman said, "All right, climb aboard."

There were two wooden benches, one at each end of the small craft. Scorpio helped Leah clamber on board, as the boatman held the craft steady with his pole. She took one of the benches as Scorpio leapt agilely in and took the other bench to help balance the boat.

Without losing his aplomb, the boatman poled them across the chamber and through an arched doorway. In the next chamber he fetched up at a sort of pier, where

Scorpio and Leah climbed off and were directed to an enclosed staircase that spiraled upward.

Leah was glad that the second floor was dry. Futilely she attempted to wring out her bedraggled gown. She was beginning to realize something of what Scorpio had gone through on Earth. As a Jew, she knew what it was to have people turn aside without looking at her, but it was something else again to have someone stare with a barely repressed look of horror. After getting this reception over and over, one would surely begin to feel monstrous.

Scorpio had to repeat his request to another functionary in a gold-buttoned vest. At last they were led to an inner chamber whose walls were overspread with a netlike device that held literally thousands of cylindrical shapes made of a glassy substance.

"The TimeKeeper's private library," said Scorpio reverently. "It was destroyed in one of the Hunters' early raids on Hsarlik. They wanted to make sure there was nothing left to remember."

"But what about Verlane?"

"He died of old age, I believe, long before the Hunters arrived."

As if he were a ghost, called up by Scorpio's recollection, Verlane stepped silently into the room. He had the natural slenderness of all Aquay, but sedentary living had given him a small potbelly and stooped posture. Scorpio made a quick head-bobbing gesture that Leah read as a sign of respect for the wise elder.

"Speak, Seeker of Knowledge," said Verlane, stretching out one web-fingered hand toward Scorpio. He was self-contained enough not to stare boldly at Leah, but she had seen the initial startlement he had covered so quickly.

"This may be difficult for you to believe, TimeKeeper," said Scorpio, "but I come from the future."

Verlane was silent, waiting for Scorpio to continue, but the glance he had given to Leah was at once fleeting and astute.

"We came using this orb device," said Scorpio, removing the orb from the pouch at his belt.

The look Verlane gave the orb was direct and somewhat surprised. Scorpio began to tell his story, and the old Aquay peered at him and nodded from time to time.

"You haven't seen what I have," said Scorpio, ending his perhaps unbelievable tale, "the proud Aquay reduced to the status of mindless slaves. If it's possible I have to find a way to move time itself in its course. I need a plan, something that would bring the Aquay together and restore their spirit."

"A very interesting puzzle, indeed," said Verlane. "You have the power to move in time and space, yet the course of history seems inexorable. What would be the fulcrum upon which the weight of time itself might be moved?"

We're wasting our time here, thought Leah. *The old Aquay is so immersed in his books, he calls the downfall of a race an interesting puzzle to be solved. Or else he considers Scorpio a charlatan and is toying with him.*

A few moments passed in uncomfortable silence as Verlane withdrew inside himself, tapped his fingers on the desktop, hummed an atonal little melody.

"Ah," he said at last. "Perhaps . . ." He rose from his chair and strode to the wall. Pulling on one of the lines of the netting, he lowered a cylinder to within his reach.

As he brought it over, Leah saw that it was a smooth, conical shell and that tiny characters had been etched in a spiral around its surface.

"Have you ever heard of Raniki, the Sea Dragon and his Unblinking Eye?" asked Verlane.

"Yes, I think so," said Scorpio. "The name is in a prayer for the dead I learned a long time ago, but I don't know who Raniki is, or what is meant by an Unblinking Eye."

"Raniki was a culture hero of the Aquay. He came from The Deeps and taught us to cultivate the sea-chert to form our dwellings and to grow and harvest the edible polyps. I'll admit I'm not too certain about what was meant by an Unblinking Eye. It was your device that gave me the idea. Its light never wavers."

"But what have a lot of old legends to do with what's happening to us now? No one believes anymore in mythical heroes."

"If they do not, then your future is certainly a barren place," said Verlane. "I'm glad I don't have to live in it. That's what's lacking—a hero to let the people know who they are."

"Yes," said Leah suddenly. "Like Samson or David. Like Moses!" Verlane looked startled as she spoke. It was as if he didn't expect something so outlandish to have thoughts.

"Are you saying I must go back in time to locate this Raniki? What if he never existed in the first place?"

"That would be impossibly awkward," said Verlane. "No, I'm afraid you have to *become* Raniki."

"It could work," said Leah. "You'd be like a spark jumping from point to point throughout the past, until finally—an explosion!"

"This wasn't what I came to you for," said Scorpio to Verlane. "There has to be some other way. I'm not a hero. I've barely learned to handle the orb. How can the fate of my people depend entirely on me?"

"Moses wasn't too happy himself when the voice spoke from the burning bush," said Leah. "He stuttered, you know. But somehow he managed, so you'll have to do the same."

"One major problem as I see it," said Verlane, "is that whenever you travel to a new era in time, you'll be faced with a language barrier."

"That won't be a problem," said Scorpio. "Our orbcraft sleep-teaches us whatever language is spoken at our destination."

Verlane looked a bit skeptical but nodded and turned to strike a small gong. When a servant arrived, Verlane gave an order for food and drink. "We must fortify ourselves," he said, "for a long night of study." He surveyed his library, pulling a string here and there to lower the books he wanted. For all his stooped posture and protruding belly, he looked quite dynamic to Leah, as if he relished the intellectual challenge. *It has to be enough for him,* Leah decided. *He won't live long enough to find out how well his plan worked.*

"The orb is back on Terrapin," said Lemus. She stood at a pedestal of black glass on which sat the last of the three orbs that had been given to the Hunters.

Nara moved her gross, toadlike form across the room to stare into the orb's golden depths. The Hunter females were more squat and stocky than the males, but Nara was even more so than the norm and bandy-legged as well. However, as Prime, she was commander of the Fortress of Chanamek, the Hunters' capital on Terrapin. Lemus, as her Beta companion, was proud of the status and it gave her the pick of all the handsomest males at mating time. Nara always cautioned her not to take males seriously; they were, at best, a diversion. Lemus was inclined to defer to Nara in everything. Betas were specially bred as half companion, half servant, and were bonded from birth to Hunters of a higher caste. It was Lemus's luck to be bonded to a Prime.

"Not only has the stolen one returned, I believe it may have merged with the one we gave Lethor," said Nara.

"But what does that mean? Has Lethor returned with both orbs?"

"Do you see him anywhere about? No, it means the fool has failed in his mission to kill that upstart Scorpio. I began to worry when Lethor and Ardon didn't return immediately to report success. How hard can it be to kill one of these Aquay worms? I see that sending a male was a mistake."

"Then that means that Scorpio has returned to Terrapin," said Lemus with an awed voice.

"He'll wish he'd stayed on whatever backwater planet he left," said Nara.

"Where is he now?" asked Lemus. "Can you tell?"

Nara squinted into orb light that made her beaked face and almond-shaped eyes appear like an expressionless mask.

"More like, when is he," said Nara. "He's gone back about five hundred years to the city of Hsarlik."

"Those old ruins?"

"They weren't ruins then, though that seems an odd place for him to make planetfall. What could he expect to find there that would help him defeat us?"

Lemus's face wrinkled as she tried to think of an answer. Nara waved her hand to let the Beta know that the question was rhetorical.

"Shouldn't we use the orb to go there and take care of him?" asked Lemus. "He may cause some mischief."

"He can do little there to harm us," said Nara. "Besides, it will soon be time for the harvest and the loading of ships and I must be on hand to see that all goes well.

Only the choicest of the crop is good enough to be sent as an offering."

"Yes, that is more important," said Lemus.

The thought of Scorpio would remain like a thorn in Nara's side for several days, not a large enough irritation to pluck out, yet never quite going away, either.

Chapter 5

Taryn took her ease and let the sling under her arms pull her through the water behind the pod-boat. She was large and vigorous and could have kept up with the large, canoelike boat easily, but they had already come a long way from shore, and she would need all her strength for the hunt. From time to time she angled her body to let head and shoulders surface so she could see the party of pod-boats as their rowers propelled them farther into The Deeps.

Each canoe had once hung on the branch of a huge torim tree, until it dried into a perfect boat shape and fell, or was picked up by an ambitious crew of krae-folk. Each clan painted their boats with different colors and designs. Several clans were represented in the hunt. This time out Taryn rode behind the boat of the Freg clan. But she owed them no loyalty; it all depended on who made the best offer.

Taryn wasn't the only leader the krae-folk had brought with them. Two others were towed behind other boats. She had been a leader of the hunt so long it didn't occur to her that this was in the least ominous. That was just the way it was done because not all leaders returned from hunting the krae.

Lolling in the water, she was becoming bored when she heard the distinctive shout, "Wa-kee, Wa-KEE!" that meant someone had sighted the humped back of a browsing krae. Taryn slipped free of the sling and began to swim swiftly past the boat. As she arced out of the water in a graceful leap, some of the male rowers made rude lip-smacking sounds and remarked on her developing body. She somersaulted in the water and came around again, this timed taking in a big mouthful of water and spraying it over the boat's side as she passed.

Shouts of surprise and a loss of rhythm in the rowing let her know that her aim was good. She knew the teasing, while crude, was all in fun, and she was proud of her healthy, maturing body, but all she had ever known was the life of a free-swimming fry. She and her friends had made fun of the land-lurchers, but soon the gills along her sides would seal shut and she'd face the prospect of becoming a land-lurcher herself.

A great many successful hunts had left her well off, with a fine krae-hide tent and a hoard of the rare pink lupine shells the krae-folk used as money. As an orphan, though, she was a member of no clan. Usually hunt leaders were orphans, with only the occasional desperate family giving up one of their children to this dangerous profession. Taryn knew of only a few leaders who had lived long enough to become an adult. *I must make every day count now,* she told herself as she swam beyond the boats.

Water in The Deeps was cold and invigorating. It awakened all her senses. Fish of exotic colors and shapes moved around her, veering away in groups as if choreographed in a bizarre ballet. Before long she spotted her quarry, a hovering dark shape of impossible size.

The krae bull reacted at once to Taryn's presence, muscles massing beneath the velvety darkness of his pelt. The saberlike teeth were so long the beast could never close his mouth completely. A humped back sloped down into a wide forehead. Slit-pupiled eyes peered out from beneath heavy brow ridges. Intelligence rather than instinct controlled that massive body. A full-grown bull was always a challenge, even if this one had no marks of hunting on him. No, he was no rogue, like Showl. Tales of the almost-legendary krae were at the back of Taryn's mind whenever she began a hunt. She thought she had caught a glimpse of Showl once, plowing through the waves, broken harpoons embedded in his thick hide, jutting in all directions, stout ropes trailing behind like streamers.

Taryn banished these thoughts. Thinking of Showl now had to be courting the worst kind of bad luck. She began to swim wildly in circles just within reach of the hovering monster, as if she were wounded and easy prey.

The bull turned lethargically about and then lunged through the water, paddlelike flippers propelling him faster and faster until he was rushing at her like a juggernaut.

Beginning leaders sometimes froze at this moment and were torn to pieces by the charging krae. Taryn was long-practiced at leader-craft, but even she understood how that hellish face with its ring of stained ivory teeth could exert a fascination. At the last possible minute Taryn stopped the awkward splashing and swam strongly in the direction of the boats.

As if enraged to see such easy prey streaking away, the krae swam after her. By swimming as hard as she could it should be just possible to stay ahead of him. The krae cut through the water only yards behind her, his mouth gaped wide to take her in. When the beast opened his saber-fanged mouth fully, he was forced to close his eyes and charge blindly, instinct overcoming his intelligence.

Led by the sound of her swimming, he followed her into the gauntlet of boats and harpooners. Taryn was too intent on her own escape to see exactly what happened, but she heard the dull pounding sounds of several harpoons seating themselves in the krae's flesh, and then the bellow of the great bull and the splashing of his struggles.

When she grasped hold of the side of a boat and pulled herself up to where she could see, the krae had been transfixed by dozens of harpoons and had passed through the gauntlet of hunters, trailing several bright floatation devices that would help them to find him when he had expended his strength.

Taryn's strength was already gone. She clung to the boat, shivering and panting, only now fully realizing how close that gaping mouth had been. But before the next hunt she would forget the horror, and remember only the excitement of a successful hunt.

Several hours later they found the floats bobbing and beside them the krae's flaccid corpse moving with the waves. They lashed it between four canoes and set out for shore where they would swarm over it with skinning knives and scrapers. Almost every part of the animal would be used in some way.

As they neared shore, Taryn began to recognize landmarks, and realized they would harbor at Crescent Lagoon. As they neared the place, the sun was setting amid bands of neon-bright color, a typical Terrapin sunset. Here and there along the shoreline torches had been set out, pinpricks of light in gathering darkness. Though the krae-folk lived a mainly nomadic life, even on land, Crescent Lagoon was one of the few places that could qualify as a settlement.

Taryn slipped free of the sling as they neared the harbor and swam in on her own. Naishe, another of the leaders who had gone on the hunt, had had the same idea. They swam along companionably through the warm water, finally thrusting their heads above the surface so that they could talk.

"Have you ever been here before?" asked Taryn. "It must be strange to live in one place all the time like they do here."

"It is. The dwellings are of wood, not of hide, but they're destroyed just as easily when the hurricane comes, or if a rogue krae raids the coast. But that's not the strangest thing about this place. The last time I was here, I kept hearing stories about a man named Raniki, who came from out of The Deeps in a golden craft. He said he came to help the krae-folk."

"The krae-folk do fine for themselves," said Taryn. She gestured toward the bulky shape of the dead bull limned against the last lingering bands of sunset. "Why should anyone think they need help?"

"I heard he was doing outlandish things. You know the wild polyps gathered by fry to add to the family's larder, Raniki said that the polyps could be seeded on rocks right in Crescent Harbor. He said there would be no need to swim far away to do the gathering."

"I suppose that's all very well for one who intends to eat nothing but polyps. I prefer a good krae-steak. But I'm glad you told me about this miracle man. He's sure to be good entertainment for our stay here."

There was a celebration on the beach that night in honor of the successful hunt. Taryn and her kind took part from the water, observing and laughing at the land-lurchers as they drank the local wine and danced clumsily in the sand, and then the fry celebrated in their own way by frisking through the waves. Afterward, they dropped through the water to wriggle about on the sandy bottom, forming nests where they could sleep peacefully till morning.

Taryn awoke early, eager for adventure. A series of deep canals penetrated the settlement, serving as a highway for pod-boats and those who preferred to swim. Taryn and her friends were able to roam about. She found the log buildings odd-looking and ugly.

"Let's go to Torim Island," said Naishe. "That's where Raniki was creating his polyp gardens. We can see if he failed or succeeded."

Taryn was curious. Since she'd been here, she had heard the Sea Dragon mentioned many times, always in awed tones. If he was a charlatan, he was a successful one. The krae-folk believed in what he said. Still, just because he could fool the land-lurchers didn't mean a quick-witted fry couldn't find him out.

As they swam, some of the younger fry were boisterous and playful, leaping full out of the water or tussling on the sandy sea floor. Taryn didn't feel like joining them in their games. She couldn't help feeling cut off from them. They acted as if this stage of life would go on forever and there was no such thing as metamorphosis.

Taryn could see that some sort of large project was going on as they drew closer to the island. Three large log buildings had been constructed, and krae-folk bustled about, carrying burdens, or strode along with three-pronged farm implements resembling tridents slung over their shoulders.

Closer in they began to pass polyp fields, row upon row of polyp plants, growing luxuriantly from rocks on the bottom. These plants looked slightly different from the wild polyps Taryn was familiar with. Nets were strung in a mazelike configuration around and over the plants. This was evidently to protect them from hungry fish.

Naishe swooped down, avoiding the nets, picked a polyp and brought it back to Taryn. She took a bite. It was much sweeter and mealier than those she had picked in the wild. *Maybe this madman's plan has merit, after all,* she thought.

"He is here! He is here!" cried a young fry swimming rapidly toward them. "Raniki, the Sea Dragon. Hurry if you want to see him. He's giving the laborers instructions about the day's work."

Taryn bobbed to the surface, gathering her skepticism. She saw an ordinary-looking krae-man standing before a crowd of workers.

"Remember that you must protect the plants from marauding fish," Raniki was saying. "The harvest is almost upon us. Our people, the Aquay, are depending on you."

He uses a strange word to describe the krae-folk, thought Taryn. *Aquay, water-born. It's weird, but I like it. Still, this is a lot of importance to put on a stringy polyp plant. How can the fate of a people depend on a vegetable?*

"Master, give us the blessing of your Eye," said a laborer.

Raniki reached for something in a pouch at his belt, and Taryn caught her breath as he produced an orb that glowed with a serene radiance.

"A trick," she said to the fry beside her, but even she wasn't so sure.

"Bless us as well," piped up Naishe.

Raniki seemed surprised to hear a voice from the water, then he approached, bearing the orb. Now that Taryn could see the krae-man up close, she realized he was not quite as ordinary as she had thought at first glance. He wore the rough krae-hide garment of her people, but he did not seem at home in it. She couldn't even explain how he differed from the krae-folk she knew, but it had something to do with the difference between the cultivated polyp and those in the wild. She began to see why people were so awed by this Raniki. There *was* something almost otherworldly about him.

As Raniki shone his golden light on the assembled fry, Taryn heard loud shouts from behind her. She heard the "Wa-kee, Wa-KEEE" call that signaled the sighting of a krae. It seemed strange to hear it this close to shore.

When Taryn turned, it was as if the chief figure of all her nightmares had materialized before her. The beast's humped back, grizzled with age, loomed large out of the water as it swam. The thing created waves that almost swamped those near the shore.

"Showl," whispered Taryn.

Showl's dark pelt was blotchy with green aader, a phosphorescent sea parasite. Old, splintered remnants of harpoons stuck out from the rogue's back at awkward angles, trailing frayed ropes. Despite these reminders of his age, Showl cut through the water with the pride of a newly launched pod-boat, uncontested mastery of the seas around him evident in his unhurried movement.

"He's going to beach!" shouted Naishe as the fry group swam in all directions. Taryn saw Showl's open maw scoop up a swimming fry as the great beast swerved just in time to keep from scraping his belly on the rocky sea bottom. Small legs kicked desperately as the mouth closed with a splintering snap. Then Taryn was too intent on her own survival to see more.

At last she scrambled to the top of a rock that jutted from the water. On the shore the workers were milling about, some brandishing their tridents like weapons.

"The crops!" shouted a worker. "Protect the crops!"

With surprise Taryn watched a mob of workers swarm into the water. By this time she was almost suffocating, her gills burning in the alien atmosphere, and she shinnied down the spire of rock. She saw Showl tearing through the nets and moving along the rows in what looked like a systematic way. His great jaws tore some plants free and his bulk crushed the rest. Taryn was amazed to see a group of workers swimming toward Showl. Suddenly a sphere appeared in the water near them. A figure was vaguely visible inside waving its arms wildly. The workers seemed cheered on by the sight. They attempted to harry the great beast with their tridents and drive him back to The Deeps, but he only turned quickly and, throwing his head, left, right, slashed into the massed workers. Blood swirled in the water like a gauzy red scarf and debris thrown up from the struggle clouded Taryn's view. She could still hear Showl swimming about among the plants, wreaking his destruction in an almost-leisurely manner.

After Showl had departed, Scorpio stood on the shore, numb with shock. Everything had happened so quickly. He had been told that rogue krae had been known to raid settlements, but he couldn't have imagined a beast of such size and ferocity. "Are you coming back with us?" asked one of the workers. Scorpio saw with shock that the man had a gaping wound along his ribs. He held it closed with one hand as casually as if he wore a torn garment.

"No," said Scorpio. "I think I'll stay here awhile. I'll be all right. You need to get back to treat that wound." He called to two others who took charge of the wounded man and led him away. After the others left he waded into the water and dived to survey the damage. It was as bad as he had feared. Row after row of his crops had been destroyed, the plants broken off near the roots. He saw little that could be salvaged. The worst was the group of laborers who had challenged Showl. Only a few had escaped, all with wounds like those of the man on the beach. They had ignored the warning he had tried to give them. It was hard to escape the feeling that his pep talk earlier, meant only to inspire the workers to do their best, might have caused the deaths. "Protect the crops," he had said, but he hadn't meant "Guard them with your lives."

Discouraged and swimming slowly toward shore, he was startled by the touch of a small cold hand on his shoulder. He saw that one of the fry had come back. He hadn't paid them all that much attention before. With the younger fry it was somewhat hard to tell, but this one was definitely a female, not that far away from her landchange. She looked exotic to Scorpio with her necklace of painted shells and the tattoos along her right shoulder and down her right arm.

"Is it all destroyed?" the fry asked.

"Yes, all," said Scorpio.

"He'll be back, you know," said the fry.

Scorpio looked puzzled.

"Showl, the krae. If you try to rebuild your farm, he'll only come back and tear it up again."

"You seem to know about him."

"I know *all* about him," said Taryn.

"Then you know more than I do," said Scorpio. "Didn't I see you before with that gang of free-swimming fry? What's your name?"

"Taryn."

Scorpio wasn't all that old, but he had a hard time recalling what it must be like to be a fry. His own upbringing had been rather strict, so he couldn't even imagine what it was like to be a free-swimmer. He had to admit there was subtle beauty in her wildness.

"I'm more saddened by the loss of life than about the crops," said Scorpio. "The workers may have sacrificed themselves because of what I said about protecting the crops."

"They believed what you said," said the fry, "about the crops being necessary to save the Aquay. Is it true?"

Scorpio was startled by the childish directness. "Yes," he said without a pause. "It's true. Both for now and for the future of our kind."

"Then their dying was done well," said Taryn with a shrug of her narrow shoulders.

Scorpio was at first shocked and then amused at her quick dismissal of what lay so heavily on his mind. She didn't really seem to be speaking out of naiveté, though. It was as if she were on closer terms with death than her age might indicate.

"You swim well for a—" she began, and then amended it to, "for an adult."

"All Aquay are strong swimmers," he said, feeling his dark mood beginning to lift. So saying, he surged ahead of her with a sudden burst of speed. Of course, she overtook him easily and turned in front of him. A slap of her webbed feet sent a spray of water cascading into his face. He heard himself laugh aloud and he sent an answering splash in her direction.

As they played, he almost recalled what it was like to be a fry. And then without explanations or goodbyes, Taryn was gone with a sudden dive, a perturbation of the water. Scorpio paddled toward shore, his responsibility bringing a solemn expression to his face again.

Leah looked up as Scorpio came in. She could tell by his expression that something disastrous had occurred. She was silent, giving him a chance to tell his story.

"All the crops were destroyed?" she asked.

Scorpio made the Aquay sign of assent.

"That's terrible, but we can plant again."

"Yes, we will plant again, but you know how intelligent the krae are. This rogue will only wait until we replant and then he'll strike again. No, the workers were right, there's only one way. We must hunt him down."

"You're going to hunt him? How?"

"The usual way, I suppose," said Scorpio.

"You suppose, *suppose*," said Leah. "You don't just suppose, you know that krae hunters use fry as bait!"

"It's not quite like that," said Scorpio. "The fry chosen as hunt leaders have few prospects. If they do well they're honored among these people."

"And if they do badly, they're torn to shreds. I can't believe you'd go along with such a cruel custom. We should be taking a stand against it, making sure it dies out."

"But it does die out," said Scorpio. "In a few hundred years from now the climate will change drastically. The krae will die, so will the pod-boat trees. A way of life will vanish from the planet." He fell silent, as if the death of a culture meant something personal to him.

Leah felt a chill to hear Scorpio say this. Sometimes when she was immersed in the moment, she forgot that she and Scorpio moved through time as if it were their element, that peoples, civilizations, could die in the time it took for them to step from *now* to *then*.

"How can you be so sure?" she asked.

"Verlane covered that in his outline of history. Don't you remember?"

"Oh, yes, now I remember," said Leah, too embarrassed to admit that she had dropped off to sleep during some of Verlane's late-night lectures. "But I still think the custom of using a child for bait is barbaric."

"I don't like it any better than you do, but it's necessary to hunt Showl if we want our project here to succeed."

"Maybe it's not. There's nothing magic about this place. We could just move on, find another sheltered cove."

Scorpio was silent as if considering this option. "I'm not sure it's that easy," he said at last. "This legend building is tricky. The krae-people will give way to other cultures, but their tales live on. I don't know if I dare let a failure of nerve become a part of my legend."

Leah saw that Scorpio was right, but it also made her realize how much the being had changed since she first met him. He had been a timorous creature, fearful of bringing attention to himself. Now, to save his people, he had to become a legend.

Chapter 6

Taryn bobbed contentedly in the still water of the cove. She heard Naishe calling for her, but was too comfortable to move or call out. The younger fry found her eventually and looked irritated. "Oh, here you are, didn't you hear me? I have some exciting news, or would you rather just loll on the beach here like a lurcher?"

That was an insult almost certain to bring on a splashing tussle between fry, but Taryn felt vaguely bored, so she only waited for Naishe to spill his secret.

"They're going to hunt Showl."

"Who is?"

"The Druin clan."

"Have the Druin elders gone mad? It would be a waste of krae-folk and boats. No one can bring in Showl."

"It wasn't the Druins who decided it, exactly." Naishe gave her a sly look. "It was Raniki. He can be persuasive, but I guess you already know that. After we saw him that day on Torim Island, you didn't stop talking about him for hours."

"Maybe I was a little impressed. Do they have a leader yet?" Taryn almost held her breath for the answer.

"No. Maybe Raniki can convince the lurchers to commit sure suicide, but where will they find a fry so foolish?"

Taryn remembered how the farm workers ran out to defend the crops from Showl. At first she had thought that they had done it for Raniki, but that didn't quite seem to be the case. It was Raniki's *idea* they were defending. A somewhat stupid idea to Taryn's mind. The polyps were all right when there was no meat in the pot, but the krae-folk had all the meat they could hunt. Still, she knew the workers weren't risking their lives for one person, but in some way for the future of the race. The Aquay, as Raniki had called them.

From his teachings, Raniki had intimate knowledge of this future world. Or at least if he didn't belong in the future, he certainly didn't belong in the world of the krae-folk either. She had been even more surprised when he had sported in the water with her like a free-swimmer. She had told no one of this. It was a moment she wanted to keep for herself.

Taryn suddenly wished Raniki had stayed in whatever strange world he had come from. Like all krae-folk she was superstitious, and there was something about this situation that seemed fated.

Later that afternoon, she was certain of it when she saw the Druin fleet enter the harbor, the stout rowers propelling the boats toward the fry encampment. Taryn watched them come, not certain that the tall, slender figure at the fore of the lead boat was Raniki, until he lifted his golden orb like a lamp to throw fiery trails across the water.

The Druins were handing gifts over the side as a way to draw the fry, cheap painted shell beads and mirrors mostly. These didn't interest Taryn now, though in her younger days she'd wrestled her companions for a chance at a shiny gewgaw. Now she only swam nearer out of curiosity, though she already knew why they were here.

"We want to talk to Taryn," said the eldest clan member leaning low over the boat's side. He was an incredibly wrinkled old lurcher with a necklace carved from krae teeth. At some point the krae themselves had claimed a souvenir; the old man's arm was missing above the elbow.

Taryn looked at him fascinatedly without speaking. She couldn't conceive of what it must be like to be so old.

"Here she is," said a fry beside her.

Taryn swam languidly over to the boat. A quick glance told her Raniki looked surprised to see her here. He knew nothing of her prowess as a hunt leader. It pleased her that he could now see how her people valued her. "You may have heard that the clan Druin has decided to hunt Showl as punishment for his depredations in Crescent Lagoon."

Taryn felt like giggling. Punishment, indeed. Showl was likely to do some punishing of his own, of anyone stupid enough to challenge him.

"What is your offer?"

"Two hundred rose lupines."

The other fry murmured among themselves. Two hundred was an impressive sum.

"Such a small price?" said Taryn. "It might be fair if Showl were a yearling bull."

"Five hundred," said the elder.

Taryn had never heard of a higher price being paid to a hunt leader. She was caught up in the moment and all the attention being given her. "Not enough."

"A place in the clan," said the elder, looking comically

shrewd, as if he knew he were making an irresistible offer.

Taryn felt her control of the situation slip. Membership in a clan was something no free-swimmer could even dream of. Taryn didn't think it had ever been done before. She looked up into the elder's wizened face as if to see if he were possibly lying, but an elder wouldn't lie about something like this. It was too serious.

Taryn looked at Raniki. "This is something that's important to you?"

"The truth is we have to hunt the beast if we are to continue to plant our crops. If there were any other way—"

"Done," said Taryn, feeling that somehow all this was fated. She couldn't have imagined that she would ever agree to hunt Showl. *Perhaps the Druins only made the offer because they thought I wouldn't live long enough to take them up on it.*

"They only talked about the best hunt leader," said Raniki, leaning over the side. "I didn't know it would be you. The Aquay owe you a debt."

"Showl isn't yet at the end of your harpoon," she said, turning to dive deeply, the other fry swimming excitedly in her wake. She had to admit she liked the feeling of power this gave her, the feeling she was at the center of momentous events. *What will there be on land to compare with this?* she asked herself.

The day of the hunt was dark and gloomy, the wind blowing dirty rags of clouds across the sun and whipping the waves to a froth. Taryn met the Druin boats at the mouth of the harbor and slipped into the sling. There wouldn't be a long journey since Showl had been seen nearby, but she wanted to conserve her strength. Two other fry she knew had been offered the second and third leader spots. Their usual boisterousness was evidently subdued by the idea that if anything happened to Taryn, they would get a chance at Showl (or he would have his chance at them).

Taryn felt strangely calm. After all, if all this was fated, what could she do about it now?

A few miles out, she heard the cry that marked the sighting of a krae, but when they came nearer, they saw that it was a small female. Taryn felt a sudden sense of relief as if she had been reprieved. *What am I doing here?* she asked herself. *Do I owe my life to some idealistic notion of the future?* She was just gathering her courage to slip free of the sling and escape when the sighting call came again.

"It's Showl!" came a cry from the boat, but she had already recognized the patchy pelt and the trailing harpoons. Now she did drop free of the sling, but not to swim away. The sight of the monster moving so arrogantly through the water and the cheers of the krae-folk on the boats drove out all fear for the moment. She again felt the weight of destiny, but now it seemed lighter. Her whole life had been dedicated to leader-craft. It was an insane occupation, but it was all she knew.

Without hesitation she swam toward the great beast and went into her wounded-fry act. Showl peered at her with his little slit-pupiled eyes and refused to be baited. *Of course, he's been around forever,* thought Taryn, *and he's been hunted by the best. This lame old trick won't work. All right, squid eater, try this!* She swam rapidly approaching the creature's huge face, then with a sudden movement she thrust out both feet and kicked him squarely between the eyes.

The whole ocean seemed to vibrate with Showl's angry bellow. Taryn swam desperately, all her former doubts threatening her concentration. It was as if she were two different beings within the same skin. One relished the chances she was taking; the other counseled caution.

Showl may be old, but I've been doing this for a lifetime, too, she told herself. She could feel the bulk of the monster behind her, drawing nearer with every movement. She knew where the boats were, but she didn't know if there would be time to reach them before Showl caught up. She knew of a desperate maneuver to gain time, but she had only heard of it. She had never thought she would need such a trick. With a sudden movement, she angled straight up and then back. With Showl's momentum, the creature's body moved rapidly beneath her, and then she was desperately reaching out for the tail fin. It worked! She found herself being towed effortlessly behind the krae. Not only did she evade being eaten, she could now rest, letting Showl do the work of moving through the water.

She was feeling quite complacent until Showl snapped his tail like a whip, throwing her off. She somersaulted through the water and Showl was on her before she had a chance to recover. The huge, open mouth rushed toward her but she managed to correct her course and swim free.

The brief free ride she had gotten from Showl gave her new energy and she swam toward the boats. She could see the bobbing keels ahead when a dark lassitude came over her. It was hopeless, after all. She was fated to die in this attempt to kill the mighty Showl. Her strokes became less energetic.

It suddenly occurred to her that death would be a convenient way to avoid becoming an adult. *Maybe that's what all this has been about,* she told herself. *I accepted this quest in the hope that I could die gloriously, instead of having to start my life over on land. The only problem is that now that I know Raniki, living on land doesn't seem such a bad idea.*

Her new self, which she now recognized as her adult self, struggled to throw off the languor that was slowing her strokes. The idea of dying gloriously now didn't compare with the idea of living under any circumstances. Even the thought of becoming old and wrinkled, like the elder, wasn't so disgusting as it had been.

Showl's teeth clashed together so close behind her that she could hear the clack of ivory, feel the surge of water against her legs. She could see the keels of the boats bobbing in the water ahead, when she felt herself choking.

The metamorphosis! My gill slits are closing. Now she understood why she had felt like two inside one body. The new was supplanting the old. Under normal circumstances when this happened she could climb up onto the beach and lie there until she had adjusted to this new mode of breathing.

Now, as ridiculous as it seemed, she was drowning.

Scorpio had been peering out across the water anxiously, even though there was nothing to see. He wondered how he could have allowed this to happen. If he had really cared about Taryn, he would have insisted on another hunt leader. The problem was that anyone wouldn't do. The Druins had praised her lavishly. To hear them talk, the only chance they had of killing Showl depended upon Taryn as leader. And it had been her decision to make. No one controlled a free-swimmer.

"Where is she?" he asked one of the rowers. "Shouldn't she be coming back by now?"

The man only shrugged.

He remembered her splashing alongside him. He couldn't bear to think of her being torn by the monster krae's fangs.

"That's enough," he said aloud, making the rowers stare at him puzzledly. "I'm calling the hunt off now!"

No one paid him any mind. Their attention was held by the speeding dark bulk of an approaching krae.

Scorpio was only interested in the tiny figure ahead of the beast. There was something wrong. Taryn was trying to swim with her head above the surface. She'd never be able to stay ahead of Showl that way.

Scorpio grasped the orb and jumped.

In the next moment he was bobbing on the surface of the water in a giant golden bubble. Taryn was about to go down, but he opened the wall of the craft and reached out to haul her inside. Showl, with mouth wide open, jumped at the orb like a fish at a lure, but his teeth only clashed together on air as Scorpio jumped back to the boat.

Must get her back into the water, he thought, lifting Taryn and carrying her toward the side of the boat. As he was about to drop her over, she choked and spat up water, and he realized that she was breathing air.

Taryn opened her eyes and looked up at him, and he became aware that he held her in his arms. Embarrassedly, he looked around for a place to put her down. She could not yet stand on her feet.

He hadn't decided what to do about this when the boat lurched suddenly, throwing them both down. There was a second wrenching impact and the bottom of the boat cracked. "Showl," said Taryn. "He's attacking the boat."

Water began to gush through the crack in the boat's bottom.

Scorpio wanted to activate the orb and carry Taryn to

safety, but that wouldn't help the crew. And it wouldn't stop Showl.

"Give me that harpoon," he said to one of the crewmen. The man only stared stupidly at him as the boat lurched and threatened to go under. He wrenched the weapon from the man's hands and activated the orb.

Showl had turned and was bearing down on the crippled boat. Those in the other boats were trying to get close enough to cast their harpoons, but there was no time. Scorpio popped into reality above Showl's back. There would be time for only one cast.

Showl roared and suddenly dived as the harpoon struck, seating itself deeply in his humped back. The rope attached to it burned Scorpio's hands as he cast it free. The float at the end of it bobbed crazily, and then disappeared, as Showl dived.

Taryn was gripping the boat's side as Scorpio returned. "He'll be back," she said.

By this time the other boats had reached them, and they pulled alongside to rescue the crew from the floundering craft.

His attention on helping transfer everyone from the sinking pod-boat, Scorpio was surprised to look up and see the float bobbing on the water nearby. Taryn saw it too and cried out as a moment later a dark bulk rose to the surface. Scorpio looked around for another harpoon, but then he saw that everyone was cheering and laughing. The lifeless body of Showl floated on the surface.

"You did it!" said Taryn. "You killed Showl."

Scorpio knew that it had been a lucky cast, aided by the fact that the orb bubble had given him a perfect angle to throw from. He said nothing as the others crowded around him. After all, why was he here except to establish himself as a hero? Getting this sort of attention had been painful to Scorpio at first, but he felt he was getting used to it. When he saw Taryn looking at him adoringly, he did become embarrassed, gruffly suggesting that the rest of the crew be transferred before their floundering boat sank altogether.

Chapter 7

Scorpio entered his headquarters at Crescent Harbor after several days of celebrating the death of the monster Showl. He wanted nothing more than to creep to his bed unseen and sleep for the next twelve hours.

"*There* you are," said Leah, every word echoing inside Scorpio's head until he grasped his head in both hands to still the ringing. The Druin had sworn to him that the polyp juice they drank to celebrate victory was nonfermented.

"If you don't mind, I'd rather not talk," said Scorpio. "I'll be fine if I can only get some sleep."

"And you deserve it," said Leah. "One of our workers told me about Showl. I guess you were right to go ahead with the hunt. They can't stop talking about your exploit."

Scorpio groaned as her voice pounded in his aching head.

"You don't need to speak," said Leah. "I just want you to hear an idea I had while you were gone. I'm redundant here. The focus needs to be on you, and I don't mind staying in the background, but you're handling everything that needs to be done here. I was thinking that even if your legend does get passed down to the present day—or the future—oh, never mind, you know what I mean, the Hunters have had control over your people for so long that they might have tried to wipe away the memory of any culture heroes."

Scorpio could only moan softly, but Leah took it as an assent, for she continued.

"Our campaign to save my father didn't work in Avignon, not because I didn't understand the process, but because the technology didn't yet exist. The watervision the Hunters use to pacify your people is quite similar to television. My friends in Cambodia explained how it worked, or they tried to. I was pretty stunned by it."

Scorpio's eyes were glazing over, so Leah hurried to finish her proposal. "You could take me to your people's future using the orb and leave me there. It's possible I could refresh the Aquay's memories of Raniki."

"It sounds dangerous," muttered Scorpio.

"Could it be any more dangerous than wandering around in your own past and hunting down mythical monsters? I think this is something I can do that would really help."

"All right," said Scorpio. "Anything. Can't I just go to bed?"

"I'm not stopping you," said Leah innocently.

The orb-craft snapped back into existence above the Hunters' capital city of Chanamek. Leah could read Scorpio's anxious memories. Before his escape, using the orb, he had sneaked into the city, using its drains. What lay above the surface was forbidding enough: a densely packed gathering of buildings that looked like featureless metal cubes, with here and there a barbed spire thrusting up. There was no touch of decoration, of any touch that one could call human. The city matched the robotlike demeanor of the Hunters themselves. Through Scorpio's thoughts Leah could see the labyrinthine turnings of the ducts and drains beneath the city and hear the thunder of machines.

Scorpio used his knowledge of the city's underside to pilot the orb-craft through the mouth of an immense duct. They emerged in an underground chamber packed with thousands of crates. There didn't seem to be anyone around. The orb came to a stop.

"If you go right through there, you should reach one of the city's quieter streets. Remember, if you have any trouble, send me a mental message and I'll be back for you."

"You see, this really won't be so dangerous after all," said Leah. "All I have to do is call for help."

"Considering how unreliable our mental bond is when we're not within the orb, it'll be dangerous enough. But if your plans fail, you can at least lie low until I return. It's a large city, and with the population being mostly the Hunters themselves, it's not well guarded, or at least it wasn't when I came before. Of course, you'll have the same problem I did when I came to your world. It was difficult to be inconspicuous. The Hunters are used to commerce with other planets on their homeworld, so you might be able to pass yourself off as an interplanetary visitor."

"I should be convincing. After all, I *am* an interplanetary visitor," said Leah. "Shouldn't you go before someone comes in here and discovers us?"

"All right, but be careful. You know what the Hunters are like."

Leah went through the dingy passage Scorpio had

pointed out and up a flight of stairs. Being inside Chanamek wasn't any more inspiring than looking at it from the outside. Everything was of dull gray metal, the buildings windowless and austere. As Leah watched, a beetle-shaped groundcar trundled by. She tried to jump back into a doorway so she wouldn't be seen by the driver, but as the machine passed, she saw that there wasn't any driver. The vehicle seemed to follow a trail of bright metal studs built into the surface of the street. It bumbled around a corner and was gone. Being in this alien environment with few resources should have been daunting, but to Leah it was a familiar situation. Leah walked along the thoroughfare, reading the small signs etched into plaques on the sides of the buildings. These identified the activity that went on there in the economical yet somewhat boring way she might have expected of a race such as the Hunters.

She heard voices and saw a pair of Hunters coming down the street in the opposite direction. She looked about, but the spare, uncluttered architecture suggested no hiding place. One Hunter, the shorter and more slender one, was holding forth in an unending speech, while the other, the larger, nodded vigorously to everything that was said and carried a huge stack of packages, while the other was unburdened. From observing the pair of Hunters that had pursued them, Leah recognized that the larger was the Beta, or servant.

The smaller one looked at Leah, who held her breath, wondering what the reaction would be. The Hunters she was familiar with were always armed and never slow to use their weapons. The smaller said something to the Beta that Leah didn't hear and in the next moment the hulking creature was approaching.

"My master wishes you to get out of sight, *shtarni*,"

said the Beta. "He feels that such as you spoils the atmosphere of this fine day and the beauty of Chanamek."

Leah became angry at the word he had called her. *Shtarni* was a word for an inferior creature, something malformed and useless.

In the next moment she realized that it was better to be insulted than shot at. She shrugged and hurried away, turning a corner so she would no longer be in sight. Scorpio was right that the sight of an otherworldling was no shock to the Hunters. Perhaps a few alien vagabonds had come with the Hunter forces to Terrapin. She wouldn't be given a welcome, but she also wouldn't cause a riot by appearing in the street, as Scorpio had almost done several times on Earth.

At the end of the growing season, Scorpio watched in satisfaction as the last of the polyps were brought up on shore by workers. The replanting had been successful, and the crops were bountiful. The workers lay the polyps on racks where they would dry in the sun, forming a stable food supply. Scorpio looked at the huddle of dingy wooden buildings that formed the settlement at Crescent Harbor.

He jumped as a hand was laid on his shoulder. He saw Taryn smiling up at him. "What are you staring at?" she asked, looking past him toward the settlement.

"I was looking at Adambra, the Greatest Among Cities," he said.

Taryn laughed, but it was an uneasy sound.

"No, it's not there yet," said Scorpio, "but it will be, someday."

"I'm not sure I like it when you seem to look into the future," said Taryn. "Even if that was what first intrigued me about you. We've accomplished so much here. The

Harvest Festival begins tonight. Can't you just be happy in the here and now?"

"I think that may just be the secret of a happy life in any time or place," said Scorpio, putting his arms around her. After her untimely metamorphosis, Taryn had soon developed her land legs and the small fin between her shoulder blades had been absorbed.

"Do you like my costume?" she asked him, stepping back to model it. The ceremonial shawl and skirt were in the clan colors of blue and gray. "Yesterday was my Naming Day," she explained. "I'm Taryn Ad-Druin now. These are gifts from my new family." She displayed several silver bracelets and a pendant in the shape of a krae.

To Scorpio she looked beautiful, but it had little to do with the new costume. He reflected he would never forget how she had gone from adolescent to adult right before his eyes. It was like being struck by lightning; he didn't think he'd ever get over it. He had looked on, somewhat disapprovingly, when Leah had taken a fancy to this or that young man on their travels through time.

Now he understood that moving from time to time, place to place, left one feeling rootless and ultimately alone. Not so surprising that one would reach out under those circumstances.

He looked at Taryn and wondered what she was thinking. Leah was the only one he had forged a psychic bond with through orb travel. Perhaps they had each had latent psi talent to begin with and the orb brought it out. He wasn't sure he wanted to know what Taryn was thinking. With the way he felt about her, that much intimacy would be frightening.

"Now I have a name," said Taryn.

"You always had one," said Scorpio. "I don't think anything sounds better than Taryn."

"I don't think you realize what that means to a free-swimmer. I have a real place among my people now. Even though I might have amassed a fortune, all I could look forward to before was the life of an outcast."

Scorpio was only half listening to her. Now that the crops were in, it was time for him to go on and polish his legend in another place. He had agonized about the decision of what to do about Taryn for days. Finally he had made up his mind. He would tell her his decision tonight at the festival.

The day waned, the sky filling with bright bands of color. From a distance Scorpio heard the music of the festival begin with the soft burbling of the waterpipes. As he and Taryn stood listening to this plaintive melody, the drums began. Taryn smiled at Scorpio and took his hand to lead him to the festival.

Fires burned high along the beach. Wildly costumed dancers pounded out a rhythm atop a huge drum made from the hide of a bull krae. Taryn led Scorpio proudly to the blue and gray tents of the Druin clan. Tables filled with food and drink were everywhere. Scorpio and Taryn enjoyed themselves for a while, then Scorpio could wait no longer to spring his surprise.

He took her aside and spoke solemnly. "Now that my work here is finished, it's time for me to move on."

Taryn looked puzzled. "We've put so much work into the crops here, and we've only just started."

"I don't mean that I'm moving on to a new location. I'll be leaving this time period altogether."

"That would be hard to believe, if anyone else but you said it," said Taryn. "I've always known there was something different, something special about you. When you talk about the future, you make everyone believe your words. But how can you think of leaving now?"

"I've been doing a lot of thinking about us. I know my future is difficult and dangerous, and I have no right to put you in danger. But I can't help it, I want you to go with me, to share my quest."

Taryn was silent.

Scorpio felt she was overcome with the idea of the two of them traveling through time together.

"I'm sorry," she whispered. "I can't go."

"What?"

"Since the Druins gave me a name I have a place here, but it isn't really that. I feared to make the leap that everyone must—the land-change. I could imagine no satisfying life on land. I would have given myself to Showl except for you. You helped me to look at the future without fear. I've gone through one metamorphosis, I can't face another."

Scorpio could do no more than hold her as she wept. Momentarily he considered throwing aside his quest, but he knew that when morning came he would board the orb-craft. Perhaps, as the krae-folk believed, these things were fated. Or perhaps he was only a fool.

Leah looked down deferentially as Hult went by and continued to pour detergent into the automatic floor scrubbers. It had taken her a long time to locate the main broadcasting station in Chanamek. It was not among the major administrative buildings, but at the end of a street that saw little traffic. It hadn't been difficult to get this menial position. There were a thousand and one chores around the station as dreary as this one.

Hult ran things here. He was an old Hunter. His chitinous skin was so cracked and broken, his face looked like a jigsaw puzzle that hadn't quite been put together right. Worse for him, he was a Beta who had somehow lost his

Alpha counterpart. Except for *shtarni* his was the lowest rung on the social ladder in Chanamek.

"Do you want your office floor cleaned?" asked Leah as she kept an eye on the flock of machines that happily buzzed and squirted and buffed away.

"I suppose," said Hult, pausing to place his thumb on the lock-plate. "But remember that this is the nerve center of the station. There is delicate equipment within, so be very careful." He opened the door and Leah led in her machines and set them to scrubbing. There was little danger of them doing damage because they had wire "feelers" that allowed them to detour around furniture. Hult must be quite familiar with them by now, so his warning was only for her benefit. Probably the idea of a lowly *shtarni* around his equipment made him nervous.

Of course he'd be even more nervous, Leah thought, *if he knew I was interested in the workings of this equipment.*

After a while Hult took no more note of Leah and the machines. He took his place and slid out something that looked like the intricate keyboard of a musical instrument. As his fingers began to play over it, a small screen before him lit up with the image of a series of waterfalls cascading down a rocky escarpment. A closer view showed water plunging into a vast, clear pool. Leah saw that the wall beside her had lit up to become an even larger screen, and it reflected the same watery images. She wasn't sure how it worked, but she was sure that Hult was controlling the images with the keyboard.

These were the water-scenes that were broadcast to the Aquay farm workers. As Leah watched, ignoring her floor-cleaning robots, she saw another image supplant that of the water. It was the face of a Hunter. Stolidly he urged the workers to ever greater feats of productivity.

After only a few minutes of the Hunter's droning monologue, the water-scenes returned. Leah's attention had been so riveted on the screen that she was surprised to hear Hult screaming. One of her cleaning robots had managed to upend itself and it was spraying water and detergent everywhere. Hult had been splattered and his skin was steaming. Leah hastened to set up the cleaner again under a barrage of Hult's shouts.

Now I'll be lucky to keep this job, she thought, *let alone learn anything about how that image-generator works.*

Chapter 8

Bodo cringed before the onslaught of the fiery-tempered old lady. It didn't matter that she was as skinny as dry reeds and that he would tower over her if he stood up. Her bird-claw hand with extended finger emphasized her points as she spoke.

"This is the third time you've broken a lamp," she harangued him. "Do you think I have unlimited shells to pay for these things?"

"I'll work, Mama," said Bodo. "I'll pay you back for the things I break. You told me to fill the lamp with oil, and all I did was pick it up." He picked up one of her clay bowls in his huge hand and as she watched his fingers crushed it, pieces falling to the floor. He looked embarrassed and got down on hands and knees to pick up the debris.

Annin shrieked. "You even break things when you show me how you break things."

"I wish I weren't so big and clumsy," said Bodo.

As he stood up, his head touched the ceiling of the hovel built of sea-grass. It was not a strong building material, but the poor had nothing else.

"Aaah, don't stand up—" began Annin, but it was too late. Bodo felt the woven sea-grass roof give way to the top of his head, and when he tried to sit down again, he unbalanced and tried to steady himself against the wall, making the whole house shake.

"I can't stand it," shouted Annin. "Get out of here now, and don't come back until you can live in my house without destroying it."

Bodo gathered his few belongings and slunk out of the house. It didn't help to hear his mother weeping as he left. Ever since his land-change Bodo had been ravenous. He had grown larger and larger and, at least it seemed to him, clumsier and clumsier.

If he reached out to open a cabinet, the handle came off in his hand. He didn't dare have any pets for fear of crushing them when he tried to give a caress. The last time he'd hugged his mother she had cried out. She told him she had had sore ribs for a month.

As he walked away he didn't want to look back, but he couldn't help it. Annin was standing there watching him with a look of helplessness. They had been desperately poor, so things would be hard for her now that she was alone. *Of course there'll be big savings in lamps and crockery,* he thought wryly.

I have to do something to improve myself, he thought. *I have to go out into the world to make my fortune. Then I'll bring all the money back to Mama and make her happy again.*

After saying goodbye to Taryn for the final time, Scorpio found himself alone on an alien shore. Clouds masked the sky and a few flurries of snow drifted into the ocean. The coast here was rocky and the sea washed in and out with a loud roaring. Temperatures had dropped in this era. Scorpio scrambled behind a boulder to get out of the chill wind.

He tried to get Taryn out of his mind without much luck. He had felt superior to Leah when she became interested in this or that young man. *A time traveler is a poor risk for relationships,* thought Scorpio. *But that doesn't mean they don't happen anyway.*

He walked a little farther along the shoreline, looking out across the choppy sea. Rising in the midst of that turbulent ocean were the towers of a mighty city—Chankra, Place of Great Wickedness. It was built of dull black chert and the years had left it crusted with algae and green aader. Scorpio thought there was a feeling of foreboding about the city, set in the midst of a stormy sea beneath banks of massed clouds.

Or at least the place has gone down in history as wicked, Scorpio told himself. *But reputation isn't everything. Maybe I'd better go see for myself.*

The orb drifted silently to earth within Chankra's massive walls. Scorpio found himself on a narrow street, but luckily no passersby had seen him land. The city looked pleasant enough except for the dull black color of its buildings. The streets were neatly kept. Nearby he saw that a work crew was picking up refuse and tossing it in a cart under the watchful eye of an Aquay in bulky tortoiseshell armor. One of the workers looked quite old, his thick skin wrinkled, his body emaciated. As he walked to the cart, he staggered and fell near Scorpio. "Help me," he cried out in a hoarse whisper.

Scorpio bent to help him up, but the guard intervened,

pushing Scorpio back. "None of your business. Get back! I tend to my crew." The guard took a whip from his belt and began to lash the fallen man with the evident intention to get him up and working again. But the man only lay where he was and moaned, too weak with exhaustion to rise.

Scorpio stepped nearer. "Can't you see he needs help?"

The guard glared at Scorpio and he tapped the whip against his leg, perhaps wishing he could be tapping Scorpio instead.

"This is not your affair, citizen. This man is a slave of the city. It appears he is worn out in service, but he will be returned to the Temple where he will be given all Honors." The man made a signal to his other workers, who loaded the fallen Aquay onto the refuse cart. It didn't seem to Scorpio this was the way to give someone Honors, but the guard gave another signal and the workers trotted away, pulling the cart with them.

Scorpio walked on, uneasy about what had happened, but realizing that he didn't yet know enough about this culture to judge it. Everything that had come down in history about Chankra as an evil city was based on rumor and conjecture. Eventually, he knew, a volcano would rise out of the sea and totally destroy Chankra. Some would call it Divine Justice.

Feeling tired and thirsty, he saw a sign offering fish and drink. As he stepped through the door, he wasn't pleased with the atmosphere, for a raucous crowd had gathered. The air was filled with the smells of unwashed bodies, rancid fish and the tang of polyp beer. He decided he'd only sit here long enough to rest and perhaps have one drink.

The Aquay who waited on him was a young giant,

though he was very timid-acting despite his size. When he brought Scorpio's drink, he set the cup down so hard, the glass vessel shattered, beer foaming all over the table and running down to puddle in Scorpio's lap.

The waiter was apologizing profusely when another Aquay in an apron and cap came up and gave the waiter a slap. "Bodo, you clumsy fool. You're going to ruin my business. Now get into the back room and help unload those casks."

Bodo cringed beneath the blow that could not have hurt him that much, Scorpio thought, given his size as compared with the tavernkeeper. The scolding sent him scrambling toward the back of the room.

"My apologies," said the tavernkeeper. "I don't know why it's impossible to get good help these days." He handed Scorpio a towel to dry himself. "Come to the table by the fire and I'll get you a new drink, on the house."

Cozily established at the table by the roaring hearth with a new drink, Scorpio thought of the chill outside and decided to linger. He had just gotten comfortable when he heard a soft voice ask, "Mind if I join you?"

If he hadn't been thinking of Taryn, he would probably have declined, since the Aquay woman standing before him had a sinister look. She had painted her face to emphasize her huge blue-green eyes and her sleek body was enclosed in a silver net. Scorpio nodded and she sat down. "My name is Cyrenne," she said.

Later, Scorpio would remember their encounter imperfectly, probably because of the drinks she encouraged him to buy, but he would remember that for a little while she assuaged his loneliness.

That was little comfort, however, as he awoke in the street with a pounding head and the feeling that he had been sleeping in ice water. That was probably because he had been, he realized, looking at the dark puddle of half-frozen water beneath him. *Loneliness makes people do strange things,* he thought, trying to rise, but finding it too difficult because of his ballooning head. He put his hands around his head to ascertain its dimensions, but it wasn't swollen to the proportions he had feared. He supposed he'd be all right if he just rose slowly.

That wasn't as easy as he'd thought because of the street's icy surface. He slammed back down into the puddle with a splash. Desultory street traffic was just beginning as dawn broke. *Thoughtful of them to dump me on the edge of the street,* he thought. *Otherwise I'd have been run over.* By great concentration he managed to get to his feet and stay there, swaying slightly. *I have learned a great lesson,* he thought. *I'll bet Cyrenne was surprised to find I didn't have more than a few shells.* He felt for his pouch, so that he could activate the orb. *I'll go someplace warm and dry,* he thought. He exploded in panic as he realized the orb was gone and very nearly fell flat in the street again.

He looked around at the dark and lusterless buildings of Chankra. *I'm here forever!* he told himself with a horrible feeling of being trapped in a small, stifling place.

He heard a commotion and looked around to see that the tavern was still in sight. "Get out and stay out!" shouted the tavernkeeper, harrying a cringing but immense figure before him with blows of his bar towel. Bodo wasn't someone to be forgotten in a hurry, so Scorpio recognized him. "I told you if one more thing was broken you were out of a job," shouted the tavernkeeper. "You're lucky I don't sell you to the city as a slave to cut my losses. Maybe they would even do you Honors!" The tavernkeeper laughed hoarsely at this joke. "You'd be a fine morsel for Kutula."

Scorpio watched Bodo trudge dispiritedly away, and on impulse followed him. "Our luck is bad," said Scorpio, coming alongside Bodo.

Bodo started and nearly knocked Scorpio off his feet.

"Oh, I'm sorry," he said. "I can't do anything. Maybe I should just turn myself over to the Priest-Kings for sacrifice and save everyone the trouble. What was it you said, stranger?"

"I said we were out of luck," said Scorpio. "I was foolish enough to be careless with a great treasure and now I've lost it."

Bodo seemed to grow interested. "A treasure? How did you lose it?"

Scorpio embarrassedly told him what had happened with Cyrenne.

"She's one of the Night Priestesses," said Bodo. "Your treasure is no doubt in Kutula's Temple by now. I doubt you'll ever see it again. I came to the city seeking treasure, too. I wanted to bring riches back to my old ma, so she'd be proud of me. Now I'm a failure."

"I said we were out of luck, not that we were dead," said Scorpio. "We need to concentrate on the here and now. I need to get my orb back and you need—"

Bodo looked at him puzzledly.

"You need to realize how big you are."

Bodo crouched down. "Too big. Mama said I always do things with all my strength. That's why I break so much stuff. You should probably beware of being so friendly to me."

"No, don't duck down like that. Stand up. How tall are you? Six and a half feet, seven?" Haltingly, Bodo stood to his full height. Scorpio marveled at his size. Most Aquay of his own generation were fairly tall but Bodo towered over him, standing at least seven and a half feet, if not nearing eight. And he was built in proportion, far more bulky than Scorpio.

As they walked along, hugging themselves or beating their arms against their sides because of the cold, they passed an old man hacking away at lengths of firewood with an enormous ax. The implement was far too heavy for him, for when he put the ax back over his head for a stroke, it nearly pulled him backward.

"At that size, you're surely strong," said Scorpio, pausing beside the woodcutter. "Pardon me, sir, would you like to hire my friend here to finish your work?"

The old Aquay looked at them suspiciously, perhaps a bit awestruck at the size of Scorpio's companion. "I have a ton of wood here," he said. "It would take you two weeks to cut it all."

"If we should finish it in one day, would you give us that fine ax in trade?"

"Done. But you'll never finish."

"I can't do that," said Bodo. "I'd be sure to cut somebody's foot off if you put that ax in my hands."

"That may be so," said Scorpio. He waved the woodcutter to stand far back and then he began to back away himself. "But it will be *your* foot."

Bodo looked perplexed.

"Stand *up,*" admonished Scorpio. "Now grasp the ax

and try to grasp this. You will be rewarded for breaking things!"

Bodo took hold of the ax, his face creased in concentration, then he swung the ax far over his head and brought it down with a *chunk* on the log. The log split neatly in two and the old woodcutter gave a cheer. Slowly, a smile began to spread across Bodo's broad face. "I did it right!" he cried. "If Mama were only here to see this."

While Scorpio sat by, Bodo made short work of the big stack of timber. When the job was done the old man happily handed over the ax.

"I have a skill now," said Bodo. "With this ax I can go to work and earn a fortune in shells." He twirled the ax over his head as if it had been a twig. Scorpio leapt for cover and Bodo laughed.

"I didn't really have in mind a career as a woodcutter for you," said Scorpio. "You could earn money only very slowly that way. I want my orb back and I propose we storm the Temple. We should find enough treasure along the way to make it worth your while."

Bodo crouched down again. "You must be crazy to talk about an attack on the Temple. If the Priest-Kings' guard aren't enough, there's Kutula himself."

"Who is he, a warrior?"

"I'm not quite sure. Only those who are Honored know what he is, and they never return."

"Superstitious nonsense," said Scorpio. "Stand *up*, Bodo."

Bodo straightened reflexively.

"In fact, you are the shy and cowering Bodo no longer."

"I'm not?" Bodo looked puzzled again.

"No, you're, uh—uh—" Scorpio hesitated as he looked around. A merchant nearby was displaying some animal pelts out in front of his store. Whatever the beasts had been, their skins were somewhat the worse for wear; fur stuck out in all directions. When the merchant went inside, Scorpio rushed over and appropriated one of the furs. He draped it over Bodo's shoulders where it lent a barbaric effect to the brawny Aquay youth. "You're Axx," said Scorpio. "Axx, the Barbarian."

"Axx," said Bodo. "That's very—savage, isn't it?" Scorpio noticed that Axx now stood to his full height as if showing off the fur garment.

"Yes," said Scorpio. "And you don't need to worry about breaking things anymore. In fact, that's something that you want to do. And your weapon is no longer a mere woodcutter's implement. It's a battle-ax."

The merchant rushed out of his store, jabbering about thieves, but he stopped and fell silent when he saw Axx. Scorpio felt nervous. If Axx cringed now and started apologizing, all his work was in vain.

"What do you want of the Mighty Axx?"

"Nothing, sir. I was happy to be of service to such a great warrior as yourself. You're not going to rob me, are you?"

Axx laughed loudly, like a release. Scorpio supposed it was because he was realizing that he had let small people bully him all this time. "No, merchant. My partner and I would not bother with the likes of you. We're off to storm Kutula's Temple. My partner, er—what did you say your name was, stranger?"

"I didn't say, but it is Raniki."

Axx and the merchant exchanged glances. The merchant began to snicker, but then fell silent when Axx looked at him sternly. "If my friend says his name is Raniki, I believe him," said Axx.

The two of them set out for the Temple. It lay at the extreme edge of the city and was set apart from other buildings. It was a large structure with a portico held up by numerous columns of chert. "See how your ax blade does against those," said Scorpio.

"I'll probably have to sharpen it later," said Axx and swung his weapon so strongly a column cracked and toppled at the first blow. He began felling columns one after another until the roof of the portico groaned and shook. The huge brass doors of the Temple swung open and a mass of armored men rushed out.

Axx happily turned his attention to them and began to hew men instead of columns. He seemed to be holding his own, as Scorpio sidestepped the fray and entered by the open doors. A serving man who questioned Scorpio as he went up a staircase had reason to regret it, since Scorpio grabbed him by the throat.

"I want my orb back," he said, and when the servant looked confused he added, "A shining ball about so big."

The servant made the sign of assent enthusiastically, as if glad Scorpio had to take his hands off the servant's throat in order to demonstrate the orb's size.

"I saw it brought in," he said. "But it is beyond you now. It is in the Inner Sanctum, the Hall of Great Kutula." Scorpio grabbed him again and demanded where the place was.

The servant tremblingly told him. "None but the Priest-Kings ever return from there," he said.

Scorpio followed the servant's directions, coming at last to a set of double doors in blue glass. The glass was cloudily translucent and he could see within. The chamber was large, and from what he could see, empty. He caught the gleam of his orb set into a niche in the wall, decorating the place along with ceremonial masks and other objects of veneration.

The door was not locked. Perhaps the natives were frightened off with all this talk about Kutula, but he wasn't going to be. He entered and looked around for something to stand on so he could reach up and get his orb.

He noticed somewhat distractedly that the far end of the room was very dark and it slanted steeply downward. It was as if that side of the room ended in a cave or hole. A faint, foul odor wafted out from this aperture. *Kutula's lair,* he thought. *Very effective.* He was moving around the room when he began to get the feeling he was being watched, or rather he had the odd notion that it was his movement that was being perceived. He found a tall chest and began to maneuver it toward the orb. *It should be high enough,* he thought, his back to the dark part of the room.

Something struck him with terrifying force and he was thrown against the wall. His body numbed temporarily, he heard a loud scrabbling sound as of many feet moving in unison and he smelled a foul stench, many times stronger than the odor that was there before.

He rolled over and tried to see into the dimness, then he wished he hadn't because he saw a huge whitish bulk crouched there, just beyond the light given off by the orb and lamps in the room.

He could see many legs drawn up around it. These were covered in patchy dark hair, but extending from the thing was a network of long white tentacles. These were scrabbling along the floor toward him. He began to realize that the reason he wasn't moving was that one of those tentacles had stung him when it lashed out. He could feel a spreading numbness along his right side.

The tips of the tentacles reached him and played across his body as if testing whether he was still capable of movement. Then he felt himself grasped firmly and dragged across the floor. As he drew nearer he could see a face in the whitish mass, bulging eyes and a saw-toothed beak that snapped open and shut convulsively as he was drawn nearer. He imagined that beak tearing into his flesh.

A sudden crash made the tentacles stop their movement momentarily and the door splintered into thousands of glittering fragments. *Why open it,* thought Scorpio, *when it can be chopped down so dramatically.*

Not that he wasn't glad to see Axx. "Over here," he shouted, though the paralysis made his voice a thin whimper. "Watch out for the stinging tentacles!"

Axx rushed over and swinging his weapon over his head brought it down on the tentacles that gripped Scorpio. Liquids spattered and the great creature went upright on its long legs.

"That takes care of the poisoned tentacles," said Axx. "I think the thing wants to wrestle." Casting away his battle-ax, the barbarian warrior leapt toward Kutula.

With relief Scorpio felt his toes and fingertips start to tingle as feeling came back into them. *Maybe I can get up, reach the orb and be gone by the time the thing eats Axx,* thought Scorpio desperately. *He is large, so it could take a long time.*

But Scorpio's ability to move came back only in slow stages, so he was forced to watch the gargantuan wrestling match. Kutula hopped about on its long legs, occasionally snapping at Axx with its strong beak. Axx caught hold of one of the hairy legs in an attempt to trip the creature, but it only gave him a ferocious shaking and sent him tumbling to the floor.

Scorpio noticed that a number of people had now gathered in the room and were watching the struggle: guards in tortoiseshell, Night Priestesses in their seductive garb, perhaps those even more richly dressed were the Priest-Kings themselves.

Kutula was backing Axx toward the entrance to its lair when the brawny Aquay used rough spots in the wall as handholds and footholds and climbed above the great beast. He dropped down on its saclike body with his full weight crushing it onto the stone floor. The audience that had gathered cheered wildly.

By this time Scorpio was able to get to his feet. Axx came to join him, but Scorpio wanted to wave him away, so strong was the smell of dark insect ichor with which he was coated. Scorpio held his breath and greeted his friend.

"Well done, Bodo," he said.

"Axx," replied the youth. "It was a pleasant enough diversion, but you and I will have many such adventures, I promise."

"You will have many adventures," said Scorpio gently, "and I'm sure I'll read about them, someday. But I have to move on. Will you help me get my orb?"

Axx grabbed Scorpio's legs and in boosting him up to the niche boosted too high, rapping Scorpio's head smartly against the ceiling. Scorpio managed to descend dizzily with the orb in his hands.

"I know," said Axx. "Mama always said I do everything at full strength."

"Farewell, friend," said Scorpio. "You won't be offended if I don't offer my hand."

"Farewell, Raniki," said Axx. The guards and priests didn't seem to mind the smell of ichor for they were gathering around Axx enthusiastically.

"Not Raniki, Scorpio," said Scorpio with a smile, and he jumped.

Chapter 9

Scorpio stepped from the orb-craft into a scene from a storybook. Near shore stood a castle built from golden sea-chert, glistening in the sun. Through generations new sections had been built until conical towers rose far above the water's surface. The castle was perfectly reflected in the still water below it. As he watched, a rider on a giant liasn sped away from the castle at full sail. Of course he knew that legends spoke of liasns large enough to carry riders, but he was still surprised to see the real thing. The liasns he was familiar with were smaller than his hand. They had sometimes been kept as pets by fry.

The liasn's body was a translucent air sac that allowed it to ride easily atop the water. Rising from this was a long snakelike black neck topped with a tiny head with two knobbed antennae. Rather than moving at the whim of the waves, the liasn had two large winglike structures that it could raise and catch the winds to propel itself. Intricate structuring of the wing allowed it to maneuver in any direction.

A rider sat astride the base of the long neck leaning comfortably against the air sac.

"You're thinking that's an elegant way to get around," said a gravelly voice from behind him. Someone had crept up while he was taking in the scenery. "And indeed it is, but it's not for the likes of us. No, don't turn around."

Scorpio felt something sharp thrust into his ribs from behind. "I'll have that pouch at your belt."

Upon landing, Scorpio had put the reduced-size orb into his pouch for safekeeping.

"Be quick about it," said the robber as Scorpio hesitated. If he had had money, he would have been quick to hand it over, but the orb was his only way out of here. Scorpio released the pouch and reluctantly handed it over his shoulder. As he did he immediately tensed for action. The robber would almost certainly look inside since the orb wouldn't feel like a bag of gold should. Once he looked inside he would be stunned for an instant by the orb's brilliance. Or at least Scorpio hoped so. If it didn't work out that way, he'd be wearing the robber's dagger hilt like a brooch.

Hearing the faintest exhalation of surprise, Scorpio spun about and let loose with a powerful roundhouse kick. The blow went home with a satisfying *thunk*, and the bandit sprawled on the beach. Scorpio now saw that his assailant was an Aquay of somewhat more than middle years, but with a large, muscular frame and generous paunch. Most Aquay tended toward slenderness. The robber wore a tabard and breeches of darkly patterned eelskin, the usual garb for one who did rough work.

Though the blow Scorpio had delivered still made his foot and ankle tingle from the force of it, the bandit sprang to his feet. Scorpio realized that without his martial arts training he wouldn't have a chance against this man. Roaring with anger, the big Aquay charged at Scorpio, who feinted quickly, stepped aside, and as his opponent passed, swung around to catch him with a chopping blow at the back of the neck. It felled him instantly and this time the bandit showed no inclination to rise.

Keeping an eye on his fallen enemy, Scorpio began looking around the beach to see where his orb might have fallen in the struggle. He found it and secured it to his belt again.

The robber was now sitting upright and rubbing the back of his neck. Scorpio was at a loss as to what to do about him. If Scorpio delivered him to the local authorities as he supposed he ought to do, they would be sure to ask questions about Scorpio's own identity—questions he'd rather not answer.

"Well, I'm not hurt and I'm sure you've learned a lesson," said Scorpio. "I won't pursue this any further." He began to walk away along the water's edge, but to his chagrin the robber rose and began to shamble after him.

"Wait a minute," boomed the big man. "You can't just pound me into the ground and then walk away. I'm Kesla Keepswell," he said with a laugh, slapping his huge girth. "Who are you, stranger? I'd wager you'd be worth knowing."

Scorpio stopped fleeing down the beach since it wasn't doing any good. "I'm called Raniki," he said. "Sometimes Raniki of the Unblinking Eye." He gestured to his pouch where the orb rested.

Kesla began to laugh so hard he almost fell down again. "Raniki, a wonderful name," he said. "I always thought so, especially when my old pa gathered us fry together to tell the stories of Raniki. I'll never forget them. But if you're Raniki"—he made a mock-attempt to calculate the years on his fingertips—"you're over a thousand years old now, give or take a few hundred."

"If you don't choose to believe me, fine," said Scorpio and resumed his walk down the beach.

"No, wait, I believe you," said Kesla. "I was only having some fun—it's my way. Many a man's buried his own true name now that Akor's in power. See that ruin yonder?"

Not far away from the splendid golden castle he had seen upon landing were a few blackened spires jutting from the water. Scorpio wouldn't have noticed them at all if Kesla hadn't pointed it out.

"A castle of silver chert was there, even taller and more magnificent than Akor's shack. Tyranny makes an outlaw of many a good man in these times." Scorpio began feeling sorry for Kesla to have fallen from this high state. "Of course old Kesla was an outlaw to begin with," Kesla added and let go his booming laugh.

"I'm sorry to have made fun of you, friend," said Kesla. "I caught a glimpse of what was in the pouch and if you say you're Raniki I'll believe you. Are you some kind of magician?"

"Some have said so."

"That's wonderful. We need to engage Akor's Witch-Queen in a duel of magic and I think I like you. Do you want to join our outlaw army?"

Kesla was so ebullient, Scorpio felt as if he had just been volunteered for some hazardous duty. Still, he realized, if he didn't like his surroundings, he could easily orb-jump.

Scorpio gave the sign of assent and Kesla led the way into the water where he swam gracefully despite his bulk. They dived deep beneath a mazelike natural formation of chert until they emerged again into dim blue light in an undersea grotto. Several Aquay dressed similarly to Kesla came to wary attention as Scorpio entered. They carried short-swords or polyp hooks as weapons.

Kesla waved them away. "Don't just stare like yesterday's catch. Where's Landru? I think I may have found a new recruit for our band."

At the mention of the name, Scorpio realized he was in the right place. Landru had also entered the ranks of legend by opposing tyranny.

"Him? He looks puny," said a female Aquay with scarcely less bulk than Kesla.

"Have a care," said Kesla. "He managed to put me down twice with some magical way of fighting."

The others murmured and stopped scrutinizing Scorpio, turning back to their former pursuits of sharpening weapons and playing a game with dice.

They found Landru in his chambers at the grotto's deepest point. Though he was dressed as roughly as the others and was armed with a short-sword at his hip, over his eelskins he wore a handsome sea-green hooded cloak. Scorpio thought there was also something about his bearing that suggested he had once been of higher rank.

"You dared bring a stranger here?" asked Landru as Scorpio entered. "What if he was sent by Akor or his accursed woman?" Landru put his hand on his sword belt. "He'll not leave here alive if he's spying."

"He's a fighter," roared Kesla. "I can vouch for that. If he's a spy, I'll kill him myself. But for now . . ."

"All right," said Landru. "I trust your judgment, friend Kesla. It's one of the few things I do trust these days. It's just that Akor has some way of knowing my every move before I make it."

"My recruit is also a magician," said Kesla.

"All right. Sorry, stranger, that your welcome was such

a grudging one. We at least owe you the courtesy of letting you speak for yourself."

"I'm Raniki," said Scorpio, suddenly feeling like a trespasser in Landru's legend.

Landru laughed curtly. "I like him, Kesla. Boldness is what's needed around here. Raniki it is. Listen to me, then, both of you. I have plans for a new raid. I told the others of it earlier. This time we won't fail."

Akor sat enjoying his meal of polyps in wine sauce when a servant entered.

"Your Majesty, you have been summoned—" began the poor fellow, who didn't look as if he relished this duty.

Akor bellowed, "Who dares to summon a king?" and was about to throw his jeweled table dagger.

"Your wife," squeaked the servant.

Others at the table exchanged knowing glances and some even went so far as to hide smiles behind their hands.

"She says she will await you in your bedchamber on an important matter," continued the servant, now speaking very rapidly.

Akor could feel his face flushing dark beneath his thick gray Aquay skin. "Very well, but stop babbling," he admonished the servant, who scuttled away the moment he was dismissed.

Without further comment Akor left the table. Though the diners had fallen silent, he heard the sound of conversation swell again as he left the room. Without hearing what was said, he was sure he could guess at the topic: himself, the King, the most powerful being in the realm, called away by a woman. Scandalous. Still, they had no idea of what sort of woman Akor lived with.

He remembered that day three years ago. He had been locked in combat with Landru of Silverchert Castle and had not been doing *all* that badly. Losing a few battles didn't mean he would lose the war.

He had come home after one of those battles, and he was in his bedchamber about to call for a servant to help him wash away the grime of the day's fighting. There was an ornamental screen in the corner of the room, embroidered with scenes of hunting, Aquay with spears harrying a school of fish. He had thought nothing of it until from behind it someone spoke his name.

He had leapt to his feet and had half drawn his sword when the voice spoke again.

"No, you don't need to look upon me. It would perhaps be better if you did not."

Akor was no coward, but he froze. The voice had a metallic quality and seemed to issue from no Aquay throat. Also since the castle was heavily guarded, he wondered how anyone had gotten into his private chambers.

"But don't fear me, for I've come to help you. Come a little closer to the screen, and I'll tell you what your enemy was at this day."

Akor listened astounded as the voice told him Landru's latest battle strategy. It was as if whoever it was had sat at Landru's council table.

"How do I know this information isn't a pack of lies? Perhaps you were sent to confuse me, rather than help." Even as he spoke Akor had the feeling that the information he had received was accurate. From what he knew of Landru, this sounded like his sort of strategy. Still, only a fool would accept information without knowing its source.

As he made the accusation he had been creeping toward the screen. Whoever was behind it made no answer to his charge of treachery. When he threw down the screen, sword in hand, no one was there.

After a few sleepless nights debating the possibility of his own insanity, Akor characteristically decided that he was fine. He used the information the visitant had given him and wasn't terribly surprised when he won three straight battles against Landru's army. He was angry at himself for scaring away his benefactor and thought there would be no more advice forthcoming.

He was wrong about that, for several weeks later he heard the same voice issuing from a new screen. Akor's violent temper had made him tear apart the old one. The servants, who were used to this sort of behavior from their master, quietly replaced whatever had been destroyed.

"By now you're no longer questioning my credibility," said the voice. "You know what I can do to enhance your power. It remains for you to seal the pact."

Akor thought of the unpleasant result of pacts with demons as set out in the old tales. "What did you have in mind?" he asked quaveringly.

"I want to be your queen," the being said. "Yes, that would be amusing. Make the arrangements at once, and have chambers prepared for your new bride."

Akor stuttered some sort of response; he wasn't sure whether it was a yes or a no. He had been ready for the selling of souls, the draining of blood, but not the idea of a royal marriage. Since Landru had been particularly troublesome that week, Akor finally agreed.

The marriage had taken place within the month, the bride totally invisible behind yards of veiling, a costume she had insisted upon. She was still adamant that no one see her, which made Akor all the more curious. In the renovation of an old wing of the castle into the bride's apartments, he built in a secret hallway and door that only he and the builders knew of.

One night soon after the wedding, he availed himself of that hidden passage and found himself breathlessly poised outside the door. It was very late and pitch-dark in the passage. Akor couldn't decide between fear and curiosity. His new queen had been true to her word of helping him. He had driven back Landru's army and was ready to capture Silverchert. Even though she was helping him, he wasn't sure of the Queen's motives. From what she said he got the idea she considered being his queen an amusing charade, and it was obvious she had little interest in him personally. When he had asked her why she was helping him and not Landru, she had answered, "Because you are savage and stupid and will oppress your subjects."

Outside the Queen's sleeping chamber, Akor comforted himself a moment with the vision of a mythical being unlike an Aquay, yet delicate and beautiful in her own way. His dealings with the creature didn't really give him much hope for her personality, but perhaps a spiteful nature might reside in a beautiful shape.

He found that he could contain his curiosity no longer, despite what he might find in the room. Trying to be as silent as possible, he pushed the door in. There was no sound in the room and little light, but as his eyes adjusted from the utter darkness of the passage to the dimness of the room, he began to make out shapes of the heavy, ornate furniture, and then greater detail. The castle, half underneath the water as it was, utilized phosphorescent lichen as a lighting source, and there was a cluster of it on one wall.

The great bed with its clamshell headboard was occupied. Akor crept across the room, stopping suddenly when whoever was on the bed began to make a soft snoring sound. As he drew nearer he realized that light from the lichen would throw enough light onto the bed so he could see its occupant.

He never knew why he didn't scream, but only spun around blindly and fled toward the door. The sight of his queen was seared into his consciousness for all time, and he would have the door and passageway sealed up. He never tried to look upon her again.

Scorpio trod water next to Kesla as they lay in wait for the liasn caravan that would be carrying tax monies from the outlying provinces back to Akor's castle. "The beasts will be riding low in the water due to the heavy loads of gold, and so will be easy pickings," said Kesla. "Akor is robbing the country of its wealth."

"I'd think there would be more protest," said Scorpio.

"Anyone who objects to the taxes is quickly arrested and never heard from again. It's safer to pay."

"Be silent," said another outlaw nearby. "We don't want to warn them off."

The outlaw band had taken a position near a spit of land where strong winds made handling the liasns difficult, especially if they were overburdened, as would likely be the case. In the open sea, swimming Aquay had no chance of overtaking them.

Scorpio saw the outline of a liasn's sails appear in the mists, and behind it was another, and another. Between the weight of their riders and bundles attached to their saclike bodies, the beasts rode low in the water. Watching

Kesla and diving when he dived, Scorpio began to swim strongly through the choppy water. Since Scorpio was Kesla's protégé, Kesla was expected to be responsible for his training.

As they approached the liasn, Kesla looked back to be sure that the other gang members had had time to reach their targets and then signaled Scorpio to attack. Following Kesla's orders, Scorpio swam silently up under the liasn's body, to a point where he could see the rider's feet trailing in the water. Grabbing one of the feet, he yanked hard, sliding the rider off his mount. When he surfaced, he saw Kesla climbing astride the liasn, but he also saw another fleet of liasns come from behind the rocky spit of land at full sail.

"Akor's guard," shouted Kesla. "Get aboard; we must try to break through."

Scorpio scrambled up onto the slippery neck and wedged himself behind Kesla. Now the liasn was half-submerged in the water and making mournful sounds like a foghorn in distress. "This won't work," said Scorpio. He unsheathed the dagger that Kesla had lent him. "Let me cut loose the packets of gold."

"Cut them loose," said Kesla. "But don't be surprised to see an old brigand weep."

Scorpio was amazed at how swiftly Akor's troop closed the space between them. Their comrades, including Landru himself, was either still swimming after their quarry or were battling the riders for possession of the mounts.

Landru, who must have seen that the small band had no chance against Akor's larger force, shouted, "Run! Escape however you can and we'll regroup at the grotto."

Scorpio cut away the hampering packets on the liasn's

back and it sprang up higher in the water. He saw Kesla's fingers touch a rough area to either side of the beast's neck to make it move this way or that, and then they were in a race to see whether they could outrun the leaders of Akor's troop before escape was cut off.

Chapter 10

If Kesla had been a little trimmer they might have made it, but a big liasn cut across in front of them. Kesla engaged the rider with his sword, but it would only be a matter of time until a second of Akor's riders joined the first. Scorpio took out the orb, and throwing his arm about Kesla, he jumped.

The big Aquay looked stunned as a shimmering bubble enfolded him. Scorpio took him back to the grotto, where he stared around, amazed to have traveled so instantaneously. "Landru! The others!" said Kesla. "Can you rescue them as well?"

"I can try."

The orb bubble appeared in the air over the battle. At first he couldn't locate Landru in the middle of all the fighting. When Scorpio did see Landru, he was already tied to the back of an immense liasn. The orb wasn't capable of lifting such a weight, and if Scorpio went down to try to cut Landru loose, he might be captured himself.

He saw one of Landru's men swimming madly to evade capture and swooped down to rescue him. He brought the man, blinking and dripping, back into the grotto. "I'm sorry, it was too late to help Landru," said Scorpio. "And the rest have either been captured or have escaped on their own."

"You understated things when you said you were a magician," said Kesla. "I didn't realize you could do that. It should be easy to rescue Landru, no matter where they put him. It's nice to have a little magic of our own, for a change."

They waited until the survivors of the raid returned. Kesla supposed that the dungeon beneath Goldenchert was where Landru and the other captives would be held.

"Can you take us there, with that device of yours?" asked Kesla.

"I could take only one at a time," said Scorpio, "and while that would be possible, it might be better if I went alone and brought Landru back on the first trip."

"Yes, stealth is important," agreed Kesla.

"The only thing is, I'm unfamiliar with the layout of the castle and a lot of time could be wasted in popping in and out of rooms."

"Let me draw you a diagram," said Kesla. "I've never been inside Goldenchert, but all these castles were built along similar lines."

When Scorpio arrived in the castle, he expected to be in a dank, dim atmosphere in keeping with a dungeon beneath the sea. Instead the room was warm and cozy, well lit by patches of lichen. A meal was laid out on a tray. He sampled a bit of the fish and found it excellent. Kesla's diagram must have been slightly off. He was about to leave when a servant bustled in.

"Here is your equipment, Sir Korax." He laid out a full suit of silvery fish-scale armor and several handsome weapons, including a stout lance and a short-sword.

"Perhaps you should try it on now in order to be ready for the Celebratory Games tomorrow. Everyone is excited about the capture of the traitor Landru. If your suit doesn't fit, I can take it back to the Royal Armorers for adjustments."

Scorpio didn't want to alarm the castle by disappearing before the servant's eyes, so he went along with it, trying on the pieces of armor.

"Looks a little big," observed the servant.

"No, it fits fine," said Scorpio, eager to get the servant out of the room. "Just the way I like it, roomy."

"Very well, sir. I'm also commanded to tell you that Her Majesty the Queen is to confer on each participant of the Games a small token of her favor. She's now in the Receiving Room. I don't believe I need add that she doesn't like to be kept waiting. I'll be glad to conduct you there."

Scorpio sighed. It would mean more wasted time, but it shouldn't take long to complete this custom and once alone again he could activate the orb.

The servant led him to a large room with handsome murals on each wall. As he studied them, he saw a picture of a large figure with a single eye in the middle of its forehead. He was engaged in throwing a harpoon at a huge fishlike creature. Raniki's duel with the monster Showl, he decided.

The Queen sat on a throne of green glass, in which a host of tiny sea creatures swam. Her gown was heavy with pearls and golden embroidery, but she was so thickly veiled, he could get no idea of what she looked like. Of course, in the full armor including a bulbous helmet, she could see little of him, either.

Scorpio fidgeted, finally getting his chance to approach Her Highness. As he knelt to receive the favors, a tiny scrap of silk that was fastened to his helmet and one perfect black pearl, he noticed that set up behind the Queen's chair was a pedestal and on it was an orb—just like his.

The Queen is a Hunter! he thought, and confirmed it a moment later when he caught a glimpse of bright red fingertips beneath the long sleeve of her gown.

"You are dismissed," hissed a servant as Scorpio lingered, dumbstruck. Quickly he bowed himself out of her presence, trying to understand what this might mean. Once he was out of sight, he reached for the orb, and then thought better of it. He had been traced by the Hunters before through use of the orb. The more he used it, the more chance the Hunters knew where he was.

Maybe she already knows where I am, he thought, *and is just toying with me. That's what this playing at queen could be all about. No doubt guards are on the way now to arrest me.* He looked wildly around but saw only a servant carrying a tray. Nobody was interested in him at all, which probably meant the Queen didn't know he was here. *And she won't, if I don't use the orb.*

"Wait a minute," Scorpio called to the servant. "I have some important business with the dungeon keeper. Can you direct me to him?"

"Certainly, sir."

As the servant led him down a labyrinthine way to the dungeons, Scorpio tried to figure out what a Hunter was doing here, masquerading as an Aquay queen. He remembered what Landru had said about feeling that his every move was watched. An orb would be an excellent spying device, as would the Hunter's ability of nearvision.

It still didn't make a great deal of sense to him, since the Hunters were all-powerful rulers in the future time he had seen. He wondered if this were only a diversion. The Hunter did seem to be enjoying her role amid pomp and luxury. It made the stoic Hunters seem more Aquay-like to know that one of them enjoyed playing about in time this way.

But I'm not playing games in time, I'm attempting to affect the future. What can the Hunters gain by helping an oppressive ruler like Akor? Or by defeating a hero like Landru?

Suddenly it came to him. The Aquay he saw in the future were very little like the folk he knew. Though nonaggressive, the Aquay still had a great spirit of adventure and a knowledge of who they were.

The Hunters are stealing our past! he thought. *It must be done subtly since the orbs allow no major paradoxes. But the defeat of a few heroes, allowing oppression to flourish, these must have an effect.*

By now he had been conveyed to Akor's dungeons, and it was every bit as dank and airless as he had expected it to be. *Every bit as devoid of hope—* He pulled his thoughts up short. The dungeon keeper was a flabby, dirty-looking fellow who gave Scorpio a look that seemed to say he had no use for dandified knights in shiny scale armor.

"Look sharp, man, I've come for a look at Landru," Scorpio said.

The dungeon keeper scowled, but didn't quite dare refuse him. A moment later Scorpio was standing outside a barred door and confirmed that Landru was indeed in the cell. The keeper shuffled away on some other errand.

Scorpio took out the orb and let it shine into the dark cell. He wished he dared use it, but that would only put the Queen on his trail.

"Raniki," said Landru. "How did you get here?"

"No time for explanations. Tomorrow you must be ready to escape. If your door is opened and a diversion provided, do you think you could get away?"

"I would certainly do my best," said Landru.

Scorpio returned to where the dungeon keeper sat tossing his dagger at the hairy, long-legged insects that infested this place.

Scorpio paused, took out the Queen's black pearl and rolled it between his fingers. "You must be familiar with the family Korax," he said, gesturing toward the crest sewn into his armor. "A smart fellow could set himself up well, with dozens of such pearls. After all, to me, it's a mere token." He tossed the pearl to the jailor, who missed it, and then began to scrabble in the slime of the floor to retrieve it. When he found it, he looked at it closely as if he thought it false.

"What would this 'smart fellow' have to do?" the jailor asked suspiciously.

"Very little. Just open those cell doors."

The jailor guffawed.

"Oh, yes, there will be a great deal of commotion in the Gaming Arena tomorrow. The King's guard will be well occupied. So much so that a smart fellow could easily get away during the commotion."

"What sort of commotion are we talking about?"

"Leave that to me," said Scorpio. Actually, he wasn't quite sure yet what he would do.

He left, hoping that the greedy look on the face of the jailor meant something.

Scorpio found a storeroom where he could spend the night. The dust and spiderwebs told him that he probably wouldn't be disturbed. He would have liked to return to the pleasant chamber he had been in earlier, but it was probably now occupied by an irate nobleman demanding to know what had happened to his armor. With a little luck Scorpio would be able to avoid him long enough to get to the Games.

When the trumpets sounded the first call to the festival, Scorpio dusted off the armor and put it on. He joined a casual procession of other knights on their way to the arena. He went quickly to the liasn corral and a groomsman helped him choose a sturdy beast.

He had seen Kesla control one, and it didn't look too hard, but he thought he'd better practice a bit before the Games began.

It wasn't quite as easy as it had looked, he discovered. The rough patches on the liasn's neck were nerve clusters. If one touched them right, the beast was maneuvered to one side or the other. If not— Scorpio found himself whirling round and round as the beast shrieked in confusion.

By some means he managed to straighten out from the spin, but he hadn't gone far when he did something else wrong, for the beast reversed its sails and he began to go backward until he almost ran into the floating grandstand. Workers who were putting the finishing touches on the decorations shouted and cursed at him. He made the right move just in time and the liasn veered wide of the stand, into open water again.

The sight of the royal crest on the decorations also gave him just the idea he was seeking. In open water he had enough space to experiment and soon he was able to make the liasn sail about. He knew he wasn't up to the delicate maneuvers expected of an expert in jousting, but that didn't matter.

He gave himself over to enjoying the sunshine, the spray of water as he sailed and the bright colors of the clothing and decorations.

Several practice jousts had been completed by the time the King and Queen bothered to show up. They ascended to the top of the grandstand, waving to their subjects and looking as if they were in a festive mood.

Another knight sailed up to Scorpio. "Where have you been, Korax? You're up next. I can't say I envy you, having to face The Crusher. He's the Queen's favorite. But hurry and get into position. It'll all be over quickly."

Scorpio looked toward the arena and saw a huge liasn carrying an Aquay in solid black armor. "It'll be over quickly," he muttered to himself as he reluctantly took a position opposite the darkly clad knight. "More quickly than they think."

The two combatants began to sail rapidly toward each other. Scorpio saw the knight bearing down on him, long jousting lance pointed straight at his heart. At the last minute before they collided, Scorpio put his mount into a spin. His own lance made a sweeping arc, catching the knight at the back of the helmet with a loud clang and toppling him.

"Well fought," came cheers from the stands. And, "Come forth and be recognized." Scorpio needed no second invitation. Setting the sails of his beast to attain top speed he flew across the water toward the grandstand. There was a flurry of activity and shouts of warning, as some of the spectators realized his purpose. The King and Queen rose as if to flee, but it was too late.

Scorpio had his lance tipped upward as far as it would go. It was aimed at the Queen. At the last minute, Scorpio slipped from the hurtling liasn's back, so he didn't exactly see what happened.

Sounds told him a lot, though. There was a scream and a giant splash, followed by a subtle sizzling sound as the Hunter's chitinous skin reacted to a dousing. When he popped his head above water to see, a lot of guards were converging upon the place where the Queen had gone down. It was going to take them quite a while to get her out again, judging by the shouting and thrashing.

The King stood by in surprise, as if he had no idea his bride would have this reaction to water. Scorpio would have liked to watch longer, but it was time to escape.

Chapter 11

Leah moved the dustionizer across a table in Hult's office. He paid her no attention, apparently deep in thought at his complicated keyboard. After her first mistake, when she had almost lost this job, she had grown cautious. After a time Hult did not come to trust her; he learned to ignore her. But the one was as helpful as the other. When she was allowed inside the office again she tended to her business, but also managed to watch what Hult was doing.

Despite the repetitive nature of the programming on watervision, the drawing up of stored images and the combining of images to make new creations looked complex. Learning to use the device without help would be a monumental task, and that was only if she was ever given a chance to try.

Hult had finished with his work for the moment and was poking about the room as if inspecting it. Suddenly he made a sound of disgust and drew his hand back quickly. "What is *this*?" he asked.

Leah rushed to retrieve the small white block. "Oh, sorry, this is some new soap I'm trying out."

"Well, get it out of my way," said Hult.

Leah quickly pocketed the white rectangle and went about her business. When she left the room she took the square of soft substance from her pocket and almost laughed aloud to see the clear impression of Hult's thumb. It would make an excellent mold.

One night a week later Leah sat before Hult's keyboard. The mold she had made of Hult's thumbprint had worked perfectly on the lock. She wished she was having as good luck with the imaging device. She had been trying to bring up an image for hours without any success. *It's impossible,* she thought. *I have the ultimate communications device in my hands and I can't use it.*

Frustrated, she lay her head on the desk, only to rest her eyes. She wasn't sure when she fell asleep, but the sound of a door opening brought her bolt upright out of a sound slumber. Hult's stooped but immense form was silhouetted in the open doorway. "I'm sure I locked it," she heard him mutter just before he looked in and saw her at the keyboard.

It was too late to run, and it must be obvious what she was doing here. Leah decided she must risk everything on one bold move. If it didn't work, it would scarcely make things worse.

Hult came toward her, shouting and gesticulating. Instead of cringing before him, Leah stood up and met his gaze directly. "Be silent," she said in the most commanding tone she could muster. She held her breath for the result.

Hult was still shouting, but he was having trouble meeting her eyes. Slowly, his threats and accusations sputtered away into silence.

Leah hardly dared believe she had gotten away with it. "That's better," she said. "Now, sit down . . . at once!" Hult looked around the room wildly as if he wanted to bolt. This was a critical moment. His next move might be to summon the authorities or he might even use his wrist laser. Calming at last, Hult eased his stiff body down into the nearest chair where he sat primly, as if awaiting further orders.

Leah knew that this situation would seem bizarre to anyone unfamiliar with Hunter culture. Betas were born servants, bonded to a single master for life. Even though Hult's master was long dead and Hult had spent years in charge of this facility, he was still a Beta.

"Come here and help me learn to use this device," said Leah firmly.

Hult rose and obeyed.

Leah realized she had been lucky. Just because Hult needed a master didn't necessarily mean that he would accept her in that role. If she had shown the smallest sign of insecurity, the spell would have been broken.

Fortunately, no visitors ever came to the station to disturb the new roles that Leah and Hult played. Leah learned quickly from Hult's instruction.

Using stored images and a little creativity, Leah put together the image of an Aquay. He resembled Verlane a lot, Scorpio a little and even Nathan de Bernay, if only in the kind expression of his eyes.

"This is the Old Storyteller," she informed Hult where he stood at attention. "Eventually, I'm sure I'll be able to dramatize some of the tales I want to tell, but for now this is the most direct way to get my message across. I'm almost ready, but I need to know one thing."

She gestured toward the large wall monitor that reflected every broadcast sent out to the Aquay collective farms. "Are there other monitors in the Hunters' headquarters where they watch what you show the Aquay?"

"Of course not," said Hult. "Hunters can't stand the sight of all that water. It makes our skins itch. Over the years I've gotten used to it gradually since this is my job, and somebody has to do it."

Leah turned back to her keyboard. Since Hult had given himself over to her authority, he didn't seem a bit nervous about what she was doing. She flipped the switch to connect her screen to the wall monitor and at the same time to all the screens in the Aquay barracks. She could imagine the Aquay's surprise and anger to have their established routine broken.

Yan sat placidly, thinking of Voce and the children.

"Hey, where's the water?" asked one of his housemates.

"And who's that old geezer?" asked another.

Yan looked at the screen and saw that it was filled with a face. It was a well-lived-in face, Yan thought. He especially liked the kind expression of the eyes.

"Come closer, children. Gather round."

At first Yan's housemates mocked the old man and made rude noises, but Yan noticed that one by one, they did move closer. He supposed he might as well join them, even though this was most certainly another of the Hunters' ploys to play with their minds. Probably the old man would begin droning out a crop report.

"Listen now to a tale as old as The Deeps. In the time before time there was a hero called Raniki . . ."

Yan and his housemates sat enthralled until the last word was spoken. When the old Aquay's face faded from the screen, the repetitive images of water returned. Yan and his housemates, however, ignored the screen. They turned to each other, each trying to get in his own reactions to the strange broadcast.

"I think I once heard stories of this Raniki," said one.

"I wonder if the Old Storyteller will be back to tell us more," said another.

Yan couldn't remember hearing such excited conversations in the house before. On the screen the water-scenes ran on, unnoticed.

Nara moaned as Lemus put another poultice on her burned face. The dousing she had received in the time of King Akor had burned and cracked her skin over her whole body. It was, she supposed, an apt punishment for her enjoyment of her role as queen. She had an important mission in time, to make the Aquay more docile by encouraging despotic rulers. She hadn't thought she would enjoy the charade so much.

The idea of becoming Akor's queen had only been a joke at first, but the barbaric splendor of the court, the deference of the nobles, the groveling of the common folk, all these had made her savor the role of queen.

It had taken the insane knight to awaken her to reality, though she would never know what made him run amok. Akor would have to handle the problems himself; Nara had no stomach to return to that barbaric age. When she was healed, she would continue her work in other eras. She was sure she'd have her mind strictly on business from now on.

"Does that help?" asked Lemus, rearranging the cushions on Nara's air-bed.

"Ow! Stop!" shouted Nara. "Let me be!"

Lemus withdrew, looking concerned.

Missions in time were too important to share with a mere Beta, so Lemus didn't know what had happened.

Nara was left in peace for about an hour, but before she could fall asleep, Lemus came into the room again. "What is it now?" Nara snapped.

"It's one of the overseers, Lix from District 27. He says he has a report."

"Can't he use a com-unit? Why come here in person?"

"I don't know. Maybe his message is urgent."

"If he has come all this way, I suppose I must see him," said Nara. "Let him enter."

Lemus opened the door and ushered in a tall Hunter with a carrying case under his arm. He tried not to stare at Nara's cracked skin, without much success.

"What is it?" Nara asked sharply. "Some problem with the leatherleaf harvest?"

"No, that has gone well. For some reason the workers have been especially energetic. This matter I bring to your attention—"

"I hope that it's important," said Nara.

"I can't say if it is," said Lix. "I can only say it's puzzling. Graffiti has been showing up on all the walls of the collective."

"Graffiti!" raged Nara. "You came all this way to tell me about graffiti? Don't bother me with such trifles. Have the workmen repaint the walls."

"You don't understand, Prime. Discipline on our collective has always been quite strict. There has never been graffiti there at all. And this is always the same symbol. Look." Lix withdrew a sheaf of photographs from his carrying case. "You'll see that sometimes it's drawn differently, but it appears to be the same thing."

Nara peered out through the poultices at the photographs Lix held before her. The drawings were all of an ellipse with a smaller circle inside. Some of them were surrounded by rays as if to depict a flashing light.

"Why it looks like an eye," said Nara.

"Yes, that was what I thought. An eye. But I have no idea what it might mean. As a change in the Aquay's activities, it troubles me. That's why I brought it to you."

"Why should I know what it is?" shouted Nara. "This is still a trivial matter. Get out of my sight!"

Lix retreated in confusion, some of his photographs fluttering to the floor. Lemus also withdrew.

Once more left alone, Nara fell asleep, but her dreams were troubled ones. Mixed into them were the crude symbols the Aquay has scrawled on the walls of their collective. When she awoke, she called for Lemus.

"I want to know whether this graffiti has been appearing in other districts. Something about it gnaws at my mind. Contact the other overseers, but don't alarm them. Say it's only a routine check."

While Lemus was gone, Nara consulted her electronic library, giving the key word "eye."

She was still hunched over the tiny screen when Lemus returned.

Lemus looked surprised at the news she brought. "Some of the other overseers were reluctant to tell me about this since it is a breach of discipline, but I managed to get it out of them. This same symbol is being surreptitiously drawn and carved on every surface in every district."

"I've found a reference here," said Nara, "though it's rather obscure. The eye is the symbol for an early culture hero of the Aquay, Raniki, also called the Sea Dragon."

"But when we took over, the teaching of such myths was discouraged," said Lemus. "How could tales from Terrapin's dead past trouble us now?"

Nara put a fingertip to her painfully cracked forehead. "The past is never dead to those with an orb," she said. It didn't seem believable to her that a stupid Aquay could play the same game as a Hunter, but these happenings were very suspicious.

"What are you doing, Prime?"

Despite pain over every inch of her body, Nara climbed from the air-bed and opened the cabinet that held her orb. It was coruscating softly, which meant it was aware that another of its kind was being used.

"What does this mean?" asked Lemus.

"It means that I have been negligent," said Nara. "I have failed to keep track of Scorpio, who may turn out to be a serious enemy of our people. To find him we have only to follow where the orb leads." Pain made Nara sway and almost lose her balance.

"But you're not well, Prime. You must heal."

Nara allowed Lemus to lead her back to bed. Even for one who held time in her hands, Nara sensed time's evanescence. She determined that Scorpio would not slip through her fingers.

Yan walked wearily homeward. It had been a particularly grueling day. Since the harvest was going on, the workers were expected to put in longer hours. As he walked Yan looked surreptitiously around for Voce, but he didn't see her with her usual work gang. He fell into step with them and wasn't surprised to hear them discussing Raniki. There had never been such a pervasive topic of conversation at the collectives. Now when two or more Aquay gathered, they discussed the latest of Raniki's adventures as dramatized on watervision.

"It said he's coming!" one was saying.

"I know, I heard. Everyone heard, but Raniki is only a mythical character. He isn't real."

"Of course he's real. He's coming to help us break free of our alien rulers. The Old Storyteller said so."

Yan wasn't sure he could get their attention with mundane concerns. "Have any of you seen Voce today?" he asked.

Several of them gave the Aquay negative gesture, but one spoke up. "I think she fell ill last night. Of dust fever. She must have been taken to the infirmary."

The Aquay had never been meant to live in such a dry environment, so diseases such as what they called dust fever were prevalent.

Yan stood shifting from foot to foot. If he went to the infirmary to see Voce, his interest in her would no longer be a secret. Still, he didn't see how he could stay away. Maybe she needed him. At last he turned in the direction of the infirmary.

It was a busy place, staffed mostly by Aquay with a modicum of medical training and a few Hunter physicians in charge. Yan approached an Aquay med-tech behind the front desk. "I've been sent to get a report on one of your patients by my overseer. He's shorthanded and needs to know when she's coming back to work."

"What's the name and number?"

Yan gave Voce's name and assigned number. It took some time, but when the med-tech found the proper papers, he laid them on the desk. Yan quickly took note of the room number.

"You'll have to report that this worker won't be back on the job in some time. If at all. The patient is critical."

Yan mumbled his thanks and turned away before the med-tech could see his expression. He pretended to turn toward the door, and then when someone else approached the desk, he hurried down a hallway.

Room numbers went by in a blur as he sought out

Voce's room. When he found it he listened a moment at the door to make sure no one else was within.

"Voce?" he whispered, as he stealthily entered.

There was only a bed in the small cubicle, and on the bed a body, immobile and covered by a sheet. "Must be some mistake," he said and forced himself to approach the bed and lift up the sheet.

Voce was under it, looking little like herself. So still and small. Yan was suddenly sorry he had never acknowledged his love for her. Now he wanted to shout it, but this was not the time or place. It was too quiet in here, too dim, with only a ray of sunlight lying upon the sheet's whiteness. There would never be a time or place.

Leaving the room, he blundered into a med-tech who asked him what he'd been doing in there. Yan pushed him out of the way and began to run.

When he left the infirmary, the only place he could think of to go was the Aquarium. *The children are all that's left,* he thought.

When he came before the familiar tank he watched the fry swim for several moments before he realized, *They aren't mine!* He ran to the Aquarium keeper's office and pounded on the door.

"What's the matter?" asked the keeper and then gasped as Yan grabbed him and slammed him into the wall.

"The matter is my children," said Yan. "They were in that corner tank yesterday and now they're gone!"

"Why, why, I suppose they were taken away yesterday evening with others of their age and size," said the keeper, speaking rapidly with Yan's hands on his throat. "To Chanamek, of course, where they will be educated."

The keeper looked thoroughly frightened. That was Yan's only mirror of the change in himself. Now he was ready to take on the whole Hunter empire. *A little late, though, don't you think?* he asked himself. *Voce is gone and so are the children.*

He let go of the frightened bureaucrat, who collapsed onto the floor. *But maybe it's not too late. I know where the children are.*

"This is all very much against the rules," said the keeper plaintively as he left. *If I'm insane I wonder why it feels so good?* Yan asked himself. He felt he had a purpose as he headed toward the terminal. It was growing late and only one bored-looking Hunter guard was on duty. Yan knew what was in all those crates stacked on loading platforms. Leatherleaf, tons of the stuff. It was ready to be shipped to Chanamek on the Hunters' remote-controlled vehicles. *I'm ready to be shipped, too,* thought Yan as he crept toward the terminal, staying out of the light.

The guard sauntered about, making his rounds. Yan waited until the guard had turned his back and then ran to hide amid the crates. He found a wooden slat on the ground and used that to pry open one of the crates. Tamping down the leatherleaf, he made a snug nest for himself before pulling the lid back on. Then he lay back comfortably and waited. *This is an adventure worthy of Raniki himself,* Yan thought.

Chapter 12

The last drone had rumbled out of the terminal, bound for Chanamek, taking every last box of leatherleaf, including Yan's. Knots of workers lounged in the sun, unused to leisure and left at loose ends by the completed harvest. The first workers approached by the stranger were curious, yet wary. He was of their kind, but he looked different. Larger, more robust and with a sleek gray skin, he looked as if he belonged in an era when the Aquay still swam in the seas. He wore eel-skin clothing of an antique style and a green hooded cloak.

As they watched he opened a pouch at his belt and took out an object that glowed with steady light.

"What could that glowing thing be, a lamp?" asked one worker of another.

"If he needs a lamp by daylight, there's something wrong with his mind," the second worker replied with a laugh.

"You're both fools," said another of their companions.

"The Old Storyteller told us of his coming. That is his sign. The Eye of the Dragon!"

"You're right. How could we not recognize him when we've been waiting all this time?"

The word went from Aquay to Aquay. "Raniki . . . the Sea Dragon . . . his Unblinking Eye!" A crowd began to converge on the stranger. "Raniki, you've come. We've been waiting for you!"

"What's this commotion?" shouted a Hunter guard. "You workers aren't supposed to be gathering here. Get to your dorms!" The Aquay began to scatter as the Hunter approached, but the stranger stood his ground. Later, the Aquay would comment upon his courage, and the way he stood, one foot planted solidly, one slightly forward, as if he readied himself for swift movement.

"You there, you don't look like the others," roared the guard. Though in his words, he made a distinction between Scorpio and the others, by his actions he assumed this was only another timid Aquay to order about. As the Hunter reached out to grab Scorpio, Scorpio was no longer there. He had stepped back quickly, snapping out his fist to land a blow on the Hunter's wrist. This paralyzed the arm temporarily, so the laser weapon couldn't be used. Then Scorpio leapt with a surprising high-pitched cry, and his foot shot out to send the Hunter flying backward.

The Aquay stood as if dumbstruck for a moment, then the air was filled with their cheers. They gathered around the Hunter excitedly, pinning him down. One of them took the laser.

Above the tumult Nara hovered in her orb-craft. This was even worse than she had imagined. There might have been remnants of the Raniki legend left, even though the

Hunters had tried to thoroughly reeducate their charges. Legends might be powerful, but this was different. It was as if the Aquay had somehow been prepared for Raniki's arrival. The mystery nagged at her. There must be something obvious she was missing.

She now saw that she had badly underestimated Scorpio. She had thought him the very antithesis of a mythic hero, but his travels through time must have had an effect. If she didn't know better, she would have been ready to accept him as Raniki, so self-assured did he now seem.

Nara was filled with anger as the Aquay trussed up the Hunter guard and dragged him away through the dust. She touched her laser, angling the beam down toward Scorpio. It was hard to get him in her sights because of the jubilant Aquay workers gathered around him.

Then she hesitated. If Scorpio/Raniki was a powerful force alive, making him a martyr was something she didn't want to consider. No, there had to be another way to stop him.

As she was about to jump back to her headquarters, it occurred to her what was missing. The *shtarni,* Leah.

When Nara landed in her private chambers, she shouted for Lemus.

"Did you find him?" Lemus asked.

"Yes, but I don't have time to tell you of it now. We need to begin a search. We must locate every *shtarni* in the city. It can't be such a large task. There are few enough of them."

Lemus made a sound of disgust. "Who would want to know of such low and degraded creatures? I suppose there are a few who came here with us during the invasion, or stowing away on freighters. They hold menial jobs or infest the lower levels of Chanamek like vermin."

"It may be harder to trace her if she's just hiding out in the lower levels," said Nara, "but if I have an idea that she's doing more than that."

"But if Scorpio is here, shouldn't we be going after him?"

"To find prey, it's not always necessary to have it in sight," said Nara, quoting an ancient Master of the Hunt.

Leah found her mind wandering as she put the image of Raniki through his paces on the screen. She had been jumpy lately, as if it might be time to dismantle this operation and disappear. Yet there had been no trouble so far and she had no reason to think she had been discovered. As strange as it sounded, watervision was used only to placate the Aquay and was of little interest to the Hunters. It didn't even occur to them that someone could subvert their technology, as she was doing, and use it against them.

It was as if this weren't their technology at all; they were only custodians of it. It was quite puzzling, but it didn't matter, she supposed, since her work here had been so successful. She had sent Hult on a tour of the outlying collectives and from what he told her speculation about Raniki was reaching its peak.

My luck won't hold forever, she thought. *There's always the chance of an overseer going into an Aquay dorm on some errand or other. But success or failure might hinge on my staying at this just a little bit longer.*

When she finished the dramatization of how Akor was overthrown, Leah allowed the water-scenes to return. *I wonder where Scorpio is now?* she thought. She began to concentrate as she hadn't done in a long time. She wasn't sure if she reached him. Scorpio seemed very near, but as always, once away from the orb the psychic link had dwindled. It was probably best just to consider herself on her own and to continue her work here as long as possible.

Suddenly the room brightened and the orb-craft appeared. When the figure inside it stepped clear, it was a moment before Leah recognized Scorpio. The clothing was strange, but there was something different about him, something commanding in his demeanor that hadn't been there before. Leah wanted to run up and give him a hug, yet this wasn't the sort of person one did that to. She supposed that Scorpio had become who he had to, but still, it would take some getting used to.

"You did your job well," he said. "My people were waiting for me. A few more appearances among them and the revolt against the Hunters will begin."

"I'm glad you're here and that you're all right," said Leah. "I was getting awfully nervous about staying here longer."

"We can go," said Scorpio. He looked curiously at Hult.

"He's been very helpful," said Leah. "I want to erase all evidence of the programs I created. Hult isn't responsible and I don't want him blamed after I'm gone."

"All right," said Scorpio, a flash of his old self showing through the new persona. "I guess if we have plenty of anything, it's time."

"For once that's not true, Aquay," said a voice. Another orb-craft descended, placing itself between Scorpio and Leah. Inside, two forms were visible, one squat and bandy-legged, the other slightly taller and more slender.

"We couldn't bring our armies with us so we arranged for you to come to them," said the blocky female who seemed to be in charge. As she spoke, several Hunters came from a doorway behind Leah and surrounded her and Hult.

"That was why I was feeling so jumpy," said Leah. "I was being watched."

"Indeed you were, *shtarni,*" said Nara. "But I wish someone had been watching sooner. You've created quite a problem for us. But it's one which we're about to solve."

Jump, Scorpio, said Leah inside her mind, hoping that the psychic link was still working.

Scorpio clasped his orb tighter, but Nara must have been using her near-vision to catch such a subtle movement. "If you jump, she dies," said Nara. "Place the orb on the floor at your feet."

At a signal, a guard aimed his wrist weapon at Leah, his finger ready on the firing stud.

Leah, I must escape, said Scorpio, speaking mind to mind. *I haven't come this far to stop now. I have to think of my people.*

I understand, was Leah's response.

Scorpio's action came before the thought; he placed the orb on the floor. Nara scooped it up with a triumphant expression. "I told you the *shtarni* was the key to this. Imagine, giving up a kingdom for such a lowly creature."

All right, so I'm not quite the mythic hero I'd hoped to be, said Scorpio.

You still look pretty good to me.

"Guards, take both of them to cells on the lower level. I want to see or hear nothing of them, ever again."

Lemus looked at Nara. "But they're dangerous. Aren't you going to excecute them?"

"I'd like nothing better," said Nara frostily. "But the *shtarni*'s broadcasts have made that impossible. Dead, they might be enough to spark a revolution. Living, they're still dangerous, but I can only hope that given time, the populace will forget."

Scorpio discovered that technology had rendered his cell clean and dry, a step up from Akor's hospitality, or Pope Clement's for that matter, but the seamless metal walls and glaring light source made it anything but cozy. The constant pounding rhythm of the city's generators made it obvious he was in the lower level and it reminded him of the first time he had sneaked into Chanamek, armed with righteous anger and nothing else. Who would have thought it would lead to a chase across worlds and through different times.

He finished his tour of the tiny cell with the definite impression that it was escape proof. He took off his green cloak and dropped it on the cot. *So much for conquering heroes, but it was fun while it lasted. Too bad Leah didn't choose her friends more carefully.*

Immersed in a gloom of his own making even darker and danker than the sterile cell, Scorpio suddenly felt a stirring of hope. That didn't make any sense, not in this situation, then he realized it. *Leah, she and I are still in communication.*

For some reason it lifted his spirits. There didn't seem any practical application, but it still meant a lot to know he was not alone.

Yan was jolted awake. Inside the crate the atmosphere was stifling and the raw smell of crushed leatherleaf didn't help. He was half-delirious from thirst and had no idea how long he had been in the crate or if they had reached Chanamek. He could tell that the crate was moving. Even inside the box he could feel the heat of this place and smell smoke. It was hard to imagine how those details fit in.

Unable to be patient any longer, he pushed upward on the slats he had pried loose and then fastened back. The nails held a moment and then released. Yan had hoped for fresh air, but smoke and ash filled his lungs. He popped up out of the crate, choking and wheezing. If there were Hunter guards about he was sure to be sighted, but he couldn't help it.

When he looked, his first sight was of an opening filled with flame, an opening directly ahead toward which the box moved on a conveyer belt. Flames were roaring and licking the corners of his crate before he scrambled out and back to safety atop the box behind. Of course this one was moving, too. Yan dropped onto the conveyer belt and from there to the floor.

He stood staring at the long row of boxes being fed to the fire for several moments. *If I hadn't awakened—* he thought. And then, *This is the leatherleaf crop. This is what I and countless others sweated and slaved to produce all those months. And they're burning it. All of it!*

He danced around, shouting, "I told you it was worthless!" When sanity kicked in again, he belatedly looked around for guards or workmen, but no one was here. He saw only an endless conveyer belt feeding leatherleaf to the fire.

Then the stuff really was worthless, he thought, *but if farms were established, what is the crop?*

No answer to that was forthcoming, but now Yan felt very calm, as if he had been purged of his insanity. He needed water; that was the first priority. According to folk wisdom, the Aquay's sense of smell was highly developed to detect water. Living in a desert as Yan did, there hadn't been much chance to practice such a skill, but he was very thirsty now.

He began to sniff around, feeling foolish. Then he caught a whiff of something. It smelled fresh and wet. He started off, following the tantalizing scent. He was still tracking when he came to an underground launch site. The ships were not the slender passenger rockets that occasionally carried the Hunters back to their world, but large and clumsy-looking craft, freighters. He had seen their shapes passing over his collective on their way to Chanamek. He was puzzled, but the water-scent was coming from these craft.

He saw no Hunters. Here and there a small drone carried cargo or tools. Since the Hunters were not a prolific race, they relied on robots. *Then why weren't there robot workers at the collective, growing leatherleaf?*

With no one to interfere, Yan climbed the gantry of the nearest freighter. The loading door was unlocked, and when he stepped inside he realized where the water-scent was coming from. The tanks were here, packed carefully into cradles of plastic foam, and so were the fry, swimming around in confusion and bumping against the glass. The ones he saw were not his, but he felt protective toward them. All of them, packed and ready to leave Terrapin for some unknown destination.

All the time, he thought, *this was the crop the Hunters wanted. The leatherleaf was only a distraction.* Faint with hunger and thirst Yan swung clumsily down the gantry. The situation was overwhelming to someone who'd never made an independent decision in his life. He knew he must do something, but he wasn't sure what. At last he decided that the most he could do was to escape from Chanamek and tell the others. With the tension built up over the imminent appearance of Raniki, his news could be the spark that set off revolution.

To escape he needed water and food badly. He began to wander about again, trying to catch the scent of water. He caught the scent at last and followed it. This time the water was on the back of a small drone trundling down a hallway as if it had some purpose of its own. Yan dashed after it and caught up, lifting off the water jug and tipping it to his lips. It poured into his mouth, over his chin and down his front cooling him deliciously. Meanwhile the drone was moving blindly on, and the food on its back was getting away.

Yan hurried after it. It had paused beside a small slot in an otherwise featureless wall. Yan saw the drone link itself to the wall and a mechanism pushed the food tray through the slot. Yan was quick enough to grab a chunk of baked polyp just before the tray slipped inside. He was cramming the food into his mouth when he heard a shout from behind the wall.

"Hey, who's taking my food?"

It was an Aquay voice or Yan would not have answered. "It's me, Yan. Who are you and why are you behind that wall?"

"It's Scor—Raniki," said the voice. "And I'm locked in a cell. Look through the food slot and you'll see."

"Raniki, that's a good one," said Yan, leaning close to the narrow slot and looking in. At first he only saw a section of face and eyes peering back at him, then whoever was behind the wall moved so he could look inside. It was a cell all right, occupied by an Aquay in eelskin clothes. Strangely enough he did resemble the Raniki character in the watervision programs. *But what would a great hero like Raniki be doing in a cell?* he wondered.

"I have to go now," said Yan. "I have an important message to take to my people."

"Wait, don't go," said the voice. "If you're still hungry, I'll send the rest of the food out to you."

"That would be nice of you." Yan waited and the tray came out again.

Yan quickly grabbed everything edible off the tray before the drone began its trip back to whatever kitchen had sent it.

Chapter 13

Scorpio had been startled when he had seen gray Aquay fingers steal a bit of his food as the tray came through the opening. The food aperture was too small to escape through, merely a small slot for the tray, but this was his first contact with the outside world since he'd been put in here. There had to be a way to put it to use somehow. This Yan looked like a simple fellow. It didn't make much sense that he would be here in the lower levels of Chanamek.

"Yan, this mission you told me of. What is it?"

"What good would it do me to tell you? You couldn't do anything to help me, locked up as you are. Or course you couldn't do anything to hurt me, either."

"Of course not. What are you doing here?"

Scorpio listened as Yan told his story. When Yan was finished, Scorpio hit the wall with such force that his knuckles bled. "I have to get out of here!" He paced about until he had formulated a plan. "Here, put this on," he told Yan, squeezing the green cloak through the slot so

Yan could pull it through. "Now lean close and listen, here's what we'll do."

Scorpio stood tensely beside the door as he heard the commotion in the hallway beyond. "I don't understand how he could have escaped," said the gruff voice of a guard. "The locks are monitored at the main guardhouse and the door is several inches of steel. No one could break through it."

"A good thing you caught him," said the guard's companion. "He's classified as a 12A security risk."

"I thought the ranking only went to 10A."

"It did, before they admitted him and that funny-looking one with all the hair."

Scorpio heard the guards use their electronic key and the click as the bolts of the great door slid back. Scorpio cleared his mind and took a cat stance in readiness. There would be but one chance.

As the first guard escorted Yan, dressed in the green cloak, into the cell, Scorpio leapt from hiding, smashing his fist into the Hunter's face and felling him before there was even time to cry out a warning.

But the second guard saw the first fall, and if Yan hadn't grabbed him by the sleeve, he would have stepped back and slammed shut the door. With Yan holding on tenaciously, Scorpio dispatched the second guard.

Grabbing the electronic wand that controlled the doors and stripping off the guards' wrist lasers, Scorpio ran out, calling for Yan to follow. "There will be little time," he said. "The locks are monitored."

"Then where are you going?"

"I have one more door to unlock."

Leah rushed out of the cell excitedly as Scorpio opened the door. "Scorpio, I knew it was you," she said.

"How did she know that?" asked Yan. "And I thought your name was Raniki."

"No time now," said Scorpio, hustling him along.

They ran down what seemed like endless corridors with the pounding of Chanamek's machinery loud in their ears. Scorpio felt like a tiny insect darting about before the giant's shoe came down.

"Let's stop here," he said, indicating a corner half-hidden by intersecting pipes.

"Don't you think we should keep going?" asked Leah. "These corridors will soon be filled with Hunters."

"Nothing will be gained by blind flight," he said, amazed by the wisdom and dignity in the words. "Succeed or fail, we must have a plan."

Leah looked surprised and Yan handed back the green cloak, his eyes shining with hero worship.

Divested of his orb, on the run and with few resources to draw upon, Scorpio suddenly felt himself at the end of a long line of Aquay heroes. Landru had had his hour of despair; Axx was reviled; no doubt the real Raniki knew failure as well. What they would do in this situation, he was certain, was to persevere, to overcome obstacles, using whatever was at hand.

He looked around. Nothing was at hand except the guts of Chanamek, the machines that controlled the city, the planet itself.

He handed one wrist laser to Leah and the other to Yan. "You're my army," he said.

Yan looked at him adoringly; Leah just looked as if she thought he had lost his senses. "We don't even know how to use these," said Leah. "And to be honest, I'm not sure I could use it on another sentient creature."

"We're not going to use them on the Hunters," said Scorpio. "We need a diversion. For starters, how about beginning with those pipes. Stand well back; we don't know what's in them."

Leah looked dubious, but Yan was excited. Touching the firing stud, he sent a bolt lancing out toward the pipes. He had little control. The light beam scored metal walls, melted plastic tiles and finally severed a large pipe. Liquid from it hissed and spurted. It was only water.

As if not to be outdone, Leah put her beam into play to sever more pipes. When she played her beam over a switch box, there was an explosion and a shower of sparks.

"Well done," said Scorpio. He saw that a horde of small repair drones had come to try to undo the damage, but Leah and Yan kept creating new havoc while the drones trundled from one trouble spot to another.

"That's enough for now," said Scorpio. "I hear someone coming."

The Hunter technician came striding along with another troop of drones in his wake. Scorpio was pretty certain that if the robots sent back the message that they couldn't handle the problem, a real person would have to show up sooner or later.

"Stop, you are my prisoner!" said Scorpio. "Cover him," he hissed to Yan and Leah.

"What's all this about?" growled the technician. Yan sent a bolt wavering past his ankles and the Hunter froze where he was. He looked more frightened of Yan's ineptness with the weapon than of Yan himself.

"I need someone who's familiar with the layout down here," said Scorpio. "I think that'd be you."

"I don't know anything."

"Yan, prepare to fire."

"Wait, please take that weapon away from him. He could hit any one of us. I only work down here. I have nothing to do with wars topside. What is it you want of me?"

"There is a device called a forcewall," said Scorpio. "Take us to it."

"It won't do you any good," said the technician, "it's heavily guarded."

"Just take us there and leave that problem to us."

In Chanamek's heart, the apparatus that controlled the forcewall hummed contentedly. Six sleek Hunter guards patrolled the perimeters, but they had a complacent look. This was easy duty. As two of the guards paced their assigned route, a drone appeared, clicking along a metallic path. This wasn't anything out of the ordinary. Maintenance robots were common here.

But after they had passed it, the small machine left the assigned path and bumbled toward the forcewall's generator. When it rocked to a stop before that bit of equipment, another drone rolled in from the opposite side.

"Hey, what's—" shouted a guard as a third drone left the path and neared the forcewall's control panel. All three drones fired at once, cutting cables, severing cords, causing the generator to go up in a burst of flame. The guards ran about in confusion, lost in smoke and flame as the three drones rolled off in separate directions.

When he had reached a place of safety, Scorpio threw off the heavy drone disguise. He was glad when both Leah and Yan rolled in as well. They shouted triumphantly as they emerged from beneath their drones. "I don't know how you did it," said Leah, "but it was sheer genius."

"Wait," said Yan, "everything's moving too fast for me. You never really explained what that machine was for, or why we should destroy it."

"We won't know it down here," said Scorpio, "but it's going to rain. *A lot!*"

Lemus stood in the doorway of Nara's private chamber. "I hate to disturb you, Prime, but the chief guard of the lower level prison had just reported an escape."

"Then it must be Scorpio and Leah. *Why* didn't I kill them when they stood before me? Well, it's never too late to rectify a mistake. After all, what sort of mischief can they get into on the lower level?" Nara went to the pedestal where two orbs now sat. Scorpio's was now only slightly larger. She chose her own and left the other, since one orb was as much as anyone could handle at one time and, though she had experimented with it, there was no way to make one orb ride inside another.

Grasping the orb, she jumped.

On a collective farm somewhere in the Hunters' desert, Ru, an Aquay worker, lay sleeping. Her dream was of dry dirt and a blistering sun. Her dream was of black leaves blowing clear to the horizon.

Something hit the windowpane as if someone had thrown a handful of gravel. Ru was brought out of her dreams by the sound. She heard her housemates muttering and stumbling about the room.

She tried to look out the window, not knowing what was happening. There was a frightening grumbling noise from the sky. "An earthquake!" shouted someone in the room. And then the sky split from one end to another and it was as bright as day. She could see the staring eyes and open mouths of her housemates, the grimy gray walls, the watervision screen like a great blank eye. She could see the pettiness and grime of her everyday life in that brief instant when the sky cracked open.

There was more rattling against the windowpane and on impulse she threw open the window. Something hit her in the face. It was frightening at first, stinging pellets of moisture that blinded her eyes and ran down over her lips. "Water!" she shrieked. "Water from the sky!" Running crazily around the room, she urged the others, "Go outside!" Ru tugged one of them along with her, thrust her outside. Went back for another until everyone in the house was outside, dancing in the falling water like maniacs.

Ru was amazed by the freshness of it, the slick cleanliness of her skin. By dawn she was one of a great number of Aquay gathering in a field, ignoring their Hunter guards who shouted from the windows of their guardhouse. The Aquay ignored their guards' orders to go back into their dorms, inviting the Hunters to join them outside where the water was so fine. The Aquay cheered, danced, talked—and when they talked, it was of Raniki.

Freshets of water made new channels through the dusty ground. Long-lizards were washed from their holes. Creaugh sat hunched on tree branches, giving out their mournful call. Floods changed the topography of the land in a single night.

In Chanamek only a few Hunters were in the streets since the hour was so late, but the first pelting drops stopped passersby in their tracks. When the realization sank in, they screamed and began to run, taking refuge in whatever door was open to them.

In the Prime's quarters, Lemus paced about. Since she was worried about Nara, she didn't notice the first few drops spattering against the building's metal side, but when thunder rolled and the narrow windows were lit with fire, Lemus screamed and crawled under the air-bed. The storm raged on. Lightning turned the metal city into a glitter-dome of dancing reflections and water turned the streets of Chanamek into canals.

Scorpio and his army emerged from the lower level through a drain. Yan frisked through the water-filled streets like a fry. Leah only waded, but she had a triumphant look. The downpour had cleared everyone off the streets, except for an occasional drone, still going about its business, and it was an easy advance to the building that housed the Prime's headquarters.

When they reached it, Scorpio stood looking up at the top floor where the Prime's private apartments were. "I'd like to think that the place is poorly guarded because of the storm," he said. "But I don't think we can count on that."

"I'm ready to burn them down!" said Yan, waving his laser about in a way that made both Leah and Scorpio duck.

"All right, stay behind me. We're going in."

Scorpio ran toward the door, and was reassured when no one fired. The door was locked, but he let Yan, who was itching for action, burn away the lock with his laser. They startled a Hunter posted near what looked like an elevator. He got off a shot at Scorpio, but the three beams in response made him dive to the floor and scramble through an exit on the far side of the room.

Scorpio pushed buttons on the control panel until the

elevator doors opened. He couldn't believe they had gotten so far without being seriously challenged. On the top floor they crept down a hall toward an ornate golden door. It, too, was locked, but Yan's laser again provided the key.

Cautiously, they stepped inside. There was no sound. Lasers at the ready, they passed through sumptuous rooms, all dark and empty. "Where is everybody?" whispered Leah.

"The rains must be causing a crisis," said Scorpio. "Where do you suppose she's keeping my orb?"

"It's dark in here, but I see a streak of golden light beneath that door," said Leah.

The golden orb light was the first thing Scorpio saw when entering the Prime's quarters. He rushed to reclaim it. Just as he was about to touch it, light flared. Nara was returning, her ugly dark shape limned against the brightness.

Scorpio froze, the orb tantalizingly close, but still out of reach.

"Lemus, come here," Nara was saying as the craft landed. Except for orb light the room was in darkness, Nara evidently hadn't seen the intruders yet. But she would.

Yan, who was standing very near the air-bed, suddenly cried out, "Someone's got me!" Lemus, hidden under the bed, had decided to launch an attack by grabbing the closest ankle. Yan began to fire random beams, setting curtains aflame, cutting the legs off furniture, causing everyone in the room except Scorpio to seek cover.

Taking advantage of the diversion, Scorpio leapt the last few feet and grasped his orb. Leah was closest and he could only take one. He reached out to take her outstretched hand and they jumped.

Scorpio and Leah appeared again in the harvested field of a collective farm. It was a busy place, full of Aquay workers celebrating the rain. As the orb bubble burst, the crowd cried out in surprise and scattered. Then they returned and one of them shouted, "Raniki!" Others took up the cry and they gathered around.

"Tell us, what does it mean, this water-from-the-sky?" asked one of the workers.

"It means a new life for those willing to fight for it!" said Scorpio.

"Lead us, Raniki. What shall we do?"

"This is your world now. You must choose your own leader. Where are the Hunters?"

"Trapped inside by the rain," laughed a worker, pointing back toward the Hunters' barracks.

"Then make the rain your ally," said Leah. "Send workmen up to the roof to tear away the boards. Attack the Hunters while the rain falls on them."

Scorpio and Leah jumped from farm to farm, carrying his message of freedom. Crowds of Aquay rushed out to meet him, their skins drenched and almost healthy-looking, their large eyes brimming with raindrops or tears. Scorpio's and Leah's emotions melded. This was what they had fought for, what they had hardly dared hope could become a reality.

Scene layered upon scene of happy, energetic Aquay taking back their world, reclaiming their spirit. But as Scorpio stood on a hastily erected platform speaking to his people, a laser bolt seared past Leah and struck Scorpio. She saw him fall sprawling from the platform, but most importantly she felt his consciousness go out like a snuffed candle.

Nara had fired from behind one of the nearby buildings. She could not fire from inside the orb shell because it would absorb the energy.

Leah felt Scorpio's loss as keenly as if she had lost a part of herself. Though she had always doubted her willingness to use a weapon, she raised the laser, squinted along its sight and pressed the firing stud. The beam hissed out, catching Nara dead center. The Hunter crumpled, a curl of smoke rising from the body.

Numbly, Leah saw that the foolish Aquay were carrying Scorpio's body back up to the platform. Of course, she supposed it was all the same to them. A mythic hero was just as good dead as alive. *But it's not all the same to me,* she thought, tears beginning to slide down her face.

"Leave him alone," she shouted at the Aquay who were working over Scorpio as if he might somehow be revived. She was in a position to know that he was gone. She came closer to try to push the others away and saw the dark cauterized line where the beam had struck. The wound was across Scorpio's shoulders. She knelt to look closer. The beam had left a line of charred flesh, but it didn't look fatal.

When she looked at Scorpio's head, she saw a gash and a knot above his temple. *Not dead. Unconscious! And I was not skilled enough in psychic matters to know the difference.*

As the Aquay worked over Scorpio, he began to come back to his senses. "See, he's okay, or almost," said the worker. "I saw him fall off the platform and hit his head on a rock."

"Leah," Scorpio said, awakening with a start. "Nara is after us. Run! Run!"

"It's all right," Leah said soothingly. "The danger is over. We're safe now. Nara is dead." Leah felt a pang of remorse, but it was a vague and generalized feeling. She would always be guilty, but it was a guilt she could live with.

When Scorpio and Leah returned to Chanamek, they were prepared for almost any eventuality, but not for Yan, sitting behind the big desk in the Prime's Command Center. Lemus shuttled about, running his errands. She didn't seem to mind.

"Things were terribly unorganized here," he said. "I just came in and set things to rights. My first order was to unload the fry from the freighters. Eventually, we'll restore them to their parents. And of course I'll be reunited with my own fry—mine and Voce's."

Scorpio said with a shudder, "The only possible fate for those fry were the dining tables of Hunters' World."

"We would not eat your young," said an offended voice. They saw that it was Lemus who had spoken. "They were intended as an offering to vVos."

"I don't understand," said Leah. "Is that your god?"

"Gods are mythological beings," said Lemus smugly. "vVos are real."

"That means the Hunters weren't behind this plot to enslave my people," said Scorpio.

"It makes sense," said Leah. "I always wondered why the Hunters never really seemed to understand the technology they used. The machines they used weren't theirs."

"And neither were the orbs," added Scorpio.

"Well, whoever they are, these vVos aren't going to eat

my children," said Yan, looking at Lemus. "They'll have to do without your offering."

"vVos will be angry," said Lemus. The simple statement would remain in Scorpio's mind to trouble him.

"We can't worry about that," said Yan happily. "We have a world to rebuild."